A Father for Daisy

by

Jennifer Wenn

A Barnesville Novel

A Father for Daisy

Cover Art by *Kristian Norris*

The Wild Rose Press, Inc.
PO Box 708
Adams Basin, NY 14410-0708
Visit us at www.thewildrosepress.com

Publishing History
First Champagne Rose Edition, 2016
Print ISBN 978-1-5092-0655-1
Digital ISBN 978-1-5092-0656-8

A Barnesville Novel
Published in the United States of America

Dedication

To Stefan for having such a strong gene pool
that there will never be any questions
about who is the father to our foursome.

This was home to her.

Not this house. Not the woman upstairs.

No, it was these two wonderful, warmhearted people next to her that meant home to her. Andrew, her best friend, who had always been there for her and whom she knew she could trust with anything, and Alma, the warm, motherly woman who without second thoughts had opened her arms and her home for Gillian.

"I saw Daisy outside, fearlessly leading her gang toward the pond, shouting something about building a submarine to go after that big fish all the old guys insist lives there."

"I bet she is. That girl has an adventurous side I've never seen anything like. If it weren't for me holding her back with all the strength I can muster, she would have climbed Mount Everest by now."

"Why hold her back?" Andrew squinted at Gillian over his cup of coffee. "She's twelve years old. I think she's ready to face the world. If I remember correctly, we weren't sitting idly at her age."

"You don't have any children, do you?"

Andrew shook his head. "No, I don't. But that doesn't mean I don't understand the constant worry of being a parent. I'm thirty-one, and my mother still pampers me."

"I do not!" Alma gasped, outraged.

"Yes, you do." Andrew grinned, blowing his mother a kiss.

Praise for Jennifer Wenn

"Jennifer Wenn weaves a wonderful story…"
~Pauline Michael, Night Owl Romance (3.5 Stars)
~*~

"Very well-written…. The characters are so vivid. They seem about to walk right off the page."
~Maura, Coffee Time Romance and More (4 Cups)
~*~

"The plot, the characters, the love, loss, pain, and just everything about life that we know is out there is blended into the pages almost seamlessly as though they were born there."
~Valkyrie Fatality, Rockin' & Reviewing (5 Stars)
~*~

"I would definitely re-read it."
~Victoria Lane, The Romance Reviews

Chapter One

"That looks like my dimples!"

Gillian Crane sighed silently as she opened the car door, for the umpteenth time regretting the soft-hearted moment when she had told her lively daughter the truth about her father.

Daisy tumbled out from the car, her lovely blue eyes roaming the faces of the few men moving down sleepy Main Street, searching for features matching her own. Curious eyes took in the young girl's bright face, and Gillian knew she had lost the possibility of sneaking into town unnoticed.

"You got your dimples from your grandmother, remember?" Desperately trying to stop herself from throwing Daisy back into the car and leaving Barnesville and all the bad memories of her past forever, Gillian grabbed her purse. "I showed you her picture the other day, and even you can't deny you are the spitting image of her."

"And you." Daisy grinned impishly, and Gillian couldn't stop a smile of her own.

"And me. We are like three peas in a pod."

"Except for my hair, that is."

With an affectionate hand Gillian caressed her daughter's long, curly tendrils. "Except for the hair. Yours is as dark as mine is light. Considering we Cranes always have been called the Crane Vikings…"

"It must be from my father, then."

Determined, Daisy again scanned the passing men. With this fresh reminder, she now ignored all men with light hair as she continued her holy crusade of finding her father.

The thought of her twelve-year-old daughter running all over Barnesville asking indiscreet questions made Gillian feel nauseous. Why hadn't she lied when Daisy on her twelfth birthday solemnly had whispered her only wish—to know who her father was? It would have been so easy to tell a white lie, to let the girl think he'd been a soldier who died in battle, or a firefighter who had perished while saving lives.

A hero.

But no, not Gillian Crane. No, she had, without thinking twice about it, told her daughter the whole ugly truth, hoping Daisy would learn something from her mother's mistakes. What she hadn't known then was that telling Daisy the truth would be her biggest mistake ever. Because two weeks later she had received a phone call informing her that Rachel Crane, her mother, whom she hadn't seen for almost thirteen years, was dying, and Gillian was expected to come home to say goodbye.

When she'd left Barnesville all those years ago, she had vowed never to return. And yet here she was, standing on the oak-lined Main Street with her daughter's hand in hers. A daughter determined to find out who her elusive father was.

"Gilly?"

She looked up at the man who came out from the doctor's office wearing a doctor's white coat, and she frowned. There was something familiar about the handsome man's open face, his warm, dazzling smile and sparkling blue eyes under blond tresses.

"Andy?"

The hug was bearlike. She felt his chest rumble as his hearty laughter filled the air. "Silly Gilly House Mouse, it's been ages since I saw you last."

His old nickname for her, which she had loved as a child, now sounded childish and rude. But still... A shiver of delight ran through her as old feelings from her youth emerged.

Andrew Marshall had been one of her closest friends during her childhood, filling her days with laughter and fairytales. He had been a large boy with hands big as trashcan lids, a head taller than everyone else. The school bullies had loved to tease him about his size and learning difficulties, telling him over and over again to stay put at his family's farm instead of trying to achieve anything.

Too dumb, they'd said.

"Doctor Marshall, I presume?" she said with a wink and was awarded another dazzling smile.

"You remember my favorite story." He bent his head toward Daisy, his eyes checking from side to side in a secretive manner as he urged her to come closer. "When your mother and I were about your age, we loved the story of Mr. Stanley, the journalist, who found the missing Doctor Livingstone in the middle of the African jungle."

"*We* loved it?"

Ignoring Gillian's amused input, Andrew managed to look even more secretive, and the intrigued Daisy leaned closer. "Cutting his way through the dense jungle, while surviving countless attacks from poisonous snakes and terrified natives, Mr. Stanley succeeded in stumbling upon Doctor Livingstone, and as he did he said the now immortal phrase…"

Daisy, who never had been able to resist a little drama, obliged the good doctor, quirking one of her eyebrows dramatically. "Doctor Livingstone, I presume."

"Now that's a good girl who knows her history," Andrew praised, his smile warm and friendly as he straightened up.

Gillian watched him tousle Daisy's dark hair, and to her surprise the girl let him, with a bright smile. Being on the verge of teenage-hood, Daisy normally hated when people treated her like a small child, but not now.

Not with Andrew.

It wasn't so hard to figure out why, though; the girl obviously kept her options open even though Andrew was as blond as Gillian. This was going to be a long visit, Gillian thought with a deep sigh, if Daisy was going to thoroughly examine every man she met, searching for anything resembling her own person.

As she watched the two of them, she couldn't help noticing how much he had changed since she saw him last. Andrew Marshall had grown up into a formidable man, and Gillian couldn't have been happier for him. If anyone deserved to have a wonderful life, it was the warmhearted person in front of her. Once he had been clumsy, looking and behaving as inadequate as he felt, but not now. All his old insecurity was long gone; he oozed self-confidence.

"How did you know Daisy is my daughter?" she asked, trying to break her own awkwardness with this new, manly Andrew, even though she already knew the answer.

"Rachel mentioned her when I asked how you were doing nowadays. But then again, even if she hadn't I would have known by just looking at her. It's like traveling back in time, Gilly. The girl is the spitting image of you when we were kids."

"Except the hair," Daisy interjected, and he laughed again, the same hearty laughter Gillian remembered with delight.

"I must admit you are an oddity amongst the Crane Vikings. But then again, where they look a bit faded, you shine like a diamond in the rough."

"I like you."

Andrew bowed, saying with apparent sincerity, "I'm honored."

Daisy, who never lingered at anything, which Gillian at the moment found quite relieving, pointed toward Rosa's Diner. "Oh, Mommy, can we go there? The sign on the window says they have Triple Cheese Burgers. Triple Cheese!"

"I'm sorry, honey, but this is not the time. I just have to exchange a few words with Doctor Marshall here, and then we must be on our way to your grandmother's house."

Daisy pouted but didn't stress the matter. She was too intelligent to push when aware of a cause already lost. Instead she tumbled back into the car, pretending to read while her eyes continued their restless search for her father.

"I bet she's a handful," Andrew said gently, and Gillian nodded.

"Yes, she is. But then again, I wouldn't want to

change anything about her. She's perfect just the way she is."

"Is her father coming too?"

Gillian hesitated for a second. She should have known there would be questions about Daisy's father and prepared herself with some ready answers. But she had been too occupied with her turbulent feelings regarding Barnesville and her past to think twice about what to say. And now it was too late. The question was already out in the air.

"N-no," she stuttered, trying to find an easy way out. "He's not a part of our lives. Not anymore. I-it's just me and Daisy."

"Oh."

She met his warm eyes and felt a telling blush cover her cheeks. She had always been a bad liar, and she could only hope he had forgotten about it.

"How about you?" she asked, changing the subject to him, avoiding more questions needing awkward answers. "Do you have someone special in your life?"

"I most certainly do, and I am hopelessly devoted to her." His radiant happiness surrounded them like a comfortable blanket. "My little Wife is the best companion any tired man can have, always there willing to cuddle when I hit the sofa in my free time. She really is a cat's meow."

"It's lucky you're not allergic, then," she joked back and was awarded another radiant smile.

She couldn't help feeling a bit envious. She wanted a man to look as happy and content while thinking of her as Andrew did talking about his wife, the bad joke aside.

Gillian's life was all about balancing the time she

had between work and Daisy, trying not to neglect either one. Finding love was so far down on her to-do list she feared it would never happen for her.

But then again, when she left Barnesville all those years ago, she had also left her heart behind. With it had stayed all her dreams of love and living happily ever after.

Once upon a time she had believed in true love.

Once upon a time she had been in love.

"Talking about cats, Luke's back."

It was as if Andrew had read her mind, and she felt the blush deepen. She had spent her last thirteen years refusing to think about *him*, the only man who had ever been able to make her smile radiantly.

Lucas Walker.

"That's nice," she mumbled, pressing her poor purse to her chest as a shield against the old feelings awakening inside her. Resolutely she changed the subject to something more urgent, again pushing her thoughts and feelings for Luke and what he once had meant to her back into their deep hole. "Now, about my mother—I just stopped here to find out how she's doing, before I see her."

"Her heart's too tired to fight anymore. And as Rachel refuses to even consider a heart transplant or any other surgical procedure, there is not much more to do now than to wait for it to give up."

Tears burned behind her eyes as she listened to his soft voice. Of course her mother refused to do the one thing that could save her. Just the thought of having her chest opened up in front of doctors and nurses, let alone putting foreign pieces of tissue, a mechanical device, or someone else's heart inside her own body must make

Rachel sick with angst. Gillian could almost hear her mother's clipped voice saying, *"You don't know where that has been,"* as she had so often in the past, over much less important things.

"Don't let her decision get to you." Andrew put his warm hand against her wet cheek just as he had so many times before, when they were young and she'd been crying over her mother's harshness. "I think you should take this chance to be with her during her last time on earth, maybe let it heal some of those old scars you carry."

"It's been thirteen years…" Gillian started, trying to hide how returning to Barnesville had created a turmoil of old feelings inside her.

But this was Andrew.

Her childhood best friend.

The one person who always had seen straight through her, always recognizing her true feelings and not once judging her for them.

"And yet you still hurt," he interrupted gently. "I know what your childhood was like, Gilly. I know everything she said and did to you. I was there, remember? But think about this: Soon she will be gone, and then it's really too late. You will never be able to feel near her, to be able to talk to her and maybe get some answers to those questions you've asked your whole life."

They said goodbye, and as she turned the car key and the car's engine started to rumble, she made a small grimace and waved toward her old friend still standing where she left him. Somewhere deep inside she knew he was right.

But, at the same time…

How could she ever go up to her mother and ask the one question she always carried with her, the one thing she desperately wanted to know: *Why don't you love me?*

Chapter Two

The elegantly furnished bedroom was filled to its brim with visitors, all there to stand by their friend's side at her time of need.

Rachel Crane sat in her bed, a cup of steaming hot coffee in her veined, trembling hand, silently observing the surrounding commotion with unreadable eyes.

"Are you sure you don't want me to take the cup?" Gillian's concern for her mother's welfare was not well received.

"For the third time, Gillian—*no*. I'm fine as I am, thank you very much. Why don't you just leave me alone."

"But Mother…"

Rachel Crane didn't have to roll her eyes dramatically. Everyone in the room could tell how tedious she found her only child's awkward care. For a woman who had more or less ordered her daughter to come to her sickbed, Rachel Crane was behaving quite the opposite.

Gillian had been back in Barnesville for over a week, spending as much time with her mother as possible, and yet she still couldn't shake off the feeling that her mother would have preferred a scenario in which she hadn't shown up.

Daisy, who usually was a very open-minded person and never let first impressions last, refused to visit her grandmother again. When Gillian had introduced the two, Rachel had coldly ignored the girl, acting as if she didn't exist. Not once had her gaze lingered on the indignant young face which was a replica of her own.

"She's a stupid old witch, and I won't throw away my precious summer holiday on her," Daisy had sneered before rushing out the kitchen door to join her newly found friends from next door in another grand adventure.

At least that was something to be grateful for. Daisy had blended in perfectly with the neighborhood kids, as if there had been an open spot in their gang just waiting for her to claim it.

"Why don't you take the dishes to the kitchen, Gilly? I think your mother needs to rest."

Accepting the tray Alma Marshall handed her along with an escape route, Gillian felt the older woman's unspoken compassion wash over her as a snicker over her mother's open cut was heard throughout the bedroom.

Andrew's kindhearted mother had always been one of her favorite persons. When they were younger it was Alma they had gone to when they got hurt and needed comfort or when they just had a wonderful tale to tell of their adventures.

They'd never sought Rachel out.

Slowly she followed Alma, moving through the old Victorian house she'd grown up in without noticing the overwhelming grandeur. It was by far the largest house in Barnesville, built by her great-great-grandfather in an effort to show off his wealth. The locals had been, as expected, green with envy over the exquisite house, awed by its beautiful and luxurious details.

Gillian hated it.

The loneliness she had felt when, at eighteen years of age, she had arrived outside the Port Authority Bus Terminal, thrown out by a mother who had been too embarrassed to deal with her daughter's unwanted pregnancy, was nothing to what she had felt during her childhood years in this house. It was just a house with walls and a roof. Not a home.

"Don't let them get to you."

Gillian put the tray down in the spotless kitchen, accepting the cup of coffee Alma held out to her. "How can I not? It isn't as if they can't see how unwanted I am. As long as Mother behaves like I'm something the cat dragged in, why shouldn't they, too?"

"You can tell them to back off. They are grown women. They can handle it."

"Can they now?"

Alma's warm eyes sparkled with mirth. "No, I suppose not. The Barnesville Hyenas are not known for being either forgiving or respectful. If their good opinion is lost, it's lost forever, I'm afraid. And when it comes to you..." She sighed heavily. "Well, your mother seems to enjoy them belittling you, and unfortunately that makes them overdo the unwelcoming act a bit."

"What do they have against me? I was just a child when I left. I had not had time or the urge to behave as badly as they seem to think I did."

"Your guess is as good as mine." Alma shrugged. "Who knows what goes on under those perfectly styled coiffures?"

The smile they shared made her feel a bit better. Gillian knew she could never change the women's low opinion of her, an opinion she could only guess her mother had nursed with care while she had been away.

"You look good, Gillian. Andrew said you were a treat for sore eyes, and I do have to agree with him. You are more beautiful than ever."

"You are too kind." Gillian blushed, unable as always to accept praise easily.

"I have to admit I'm so proud of you." Alma sat down at the kitchen table, urging Gillian to join her. "It can't have been easy for you, all alone in New York. It would have scared me half to death, but not you. No, you managed to find both a home and a job. And when you became pregnant… Well, I think you handled that pretty good, too. Daisy is absolutely divine. A gorgeous girl."

Gillian made a little grimace. "She's the best thing that ever happened to me, but sometimes…"

"Tell me about it. I've raised three children, as you know. They are the best thing to ever happen to me, too, but at the same time I'm amazed I managed to survive their childhood."

"I can hardly handle one. Just the thought of two more sends shivers of fear down my spine."

Alma's hearty laughter, so much like Andrew's, echoed in the kitchen. "I remember one time when it became too much for me, and I yelled at my husband to drop me off at the nearest mental institution. Poor Tom, he didn't know what to do. Managing a farm and taking care of critters is nothing to him, but emotions… In the end I had him take me to town and buy me a dinner at Rosa's. A romantic evening between the two of us was all I needed to get back on track again."

"Not the most romantic setting, though," Gillian

teased, thinking of the local diner, which had looked the same since the fifties, jukebox and all.

"It didn't matter. All I needed was to feel like a woman, to feel like Alma. Thank God my mother-in-law lived with us at the farm back then. She saved my mental health many times, when Tom was too tired and worn out from taking care of the farm to be able to support me emotionally."

"You have a lovely family, Alma, and then you took in this stray every once in a while besides. Thank you for making room and time for me." Loneliness made Gillian's voice hoarse, and Alma sent her a probing gaze.

"What about Daisy's father? Doesn't he take you dancing now and then to make you forget about the monotonous round of everyday life?"

Her first spontaneous reaction was to lie, to pretend there was a man somewhere who missed them immensely but had to stay behind because of work. But then again, this was Alma, who unselfishly had dragged Gillian out of her unwanted loneliness, forcing her into the midst of her own colorful family, not once expecting anything but a hug in return. Gillian had never lied to her before, and in her heart she knew that if there was one person alive who wouldn't think less of her, it would be Alma.

"Here you are!"

The patio door flew open with a loud bang as Andrew arrived, effectively ending the awkward conversation. Feeling faint with relief at not having to tell the truth just yet, Gillian greeted him breathlessly. Coming back to Barnesville had been like riding a fast and scary rollercoaster from which she was dizzy and unable to think.

Alma scowled fiercely at her son. "Andrew Marshall, when are you going to learn how to open a door with care? You are a doctor now, and you could scare a patient half to death, crashing in like that."

"If it's a patient of mine, he or she is probably half dead anyway, so no harm done."

"Andrew Marshall!"

Ignoring his mother, Andrew turned to Gillian, winking at her with his sparkling eyes. "So, Silly Gilly, how are you surviving the Barnesville Hyenas?"

"Fine." She shrugged daintily, trying to look as if nothing bothered her, but she could tell he didn't buy her pathetic show of indifference.

Alma shook her head. "Isn't there a medicine you can give the wicked witch upstairs, something that will make her lose a little of her selfish nastiness? She's behaving dreadfully toward Gillian, and her pack does the same, too used to do as she does to think twice about it."

"Are they that bad?"

Alma nodded, her jaw clenched. "They are awful. I'm ashamed to admit I'm calling them friends."

Joining them at the kitchen table, Andrew snagged a bun from Rachel's basket and let his teeth sink into it. Alma's scowl deepened in response, clearly showing disapproval as he stole their tight-fisted hostess's food. It was a familiar look, one Alma and Andrew had shared too many times over the years and one Gillian remembered almost too well from her childhood days. Out of nowhere, for the first time since her arrival a week ago, Gillian felt a nostalgic sense of homecoming.

This was home to her.

Not this house. Not the woman upstairs.

No, it was these two wonderful, warmhearted people next to her that meant home to her. Andrew, her best friend, who had always been there for her and whom she knew she could trust with anything, and Alma, the warm, motherly woman who without second thoughts had opened her arms and her home for Gillian.

"I saw Daisy outside, fearlessly leading her gang toward the pond, shouting something about building a submarine to go after that big fish all the old guys insist lives there."

"I bet she is. That girl has an adventurous side I've never seen anything like. If it weren't for me holding her back with all the strength I can muster, she would have climbed Mount Everest by now."

"Why hold her back?" Andrew squinted at Gillian over his cup of coffee. "She's twelve years old. I think she's ready to face the world. If I remember correctly, we weren't sitting idly at her age."

"You don't have any children, do you?"

Andrew shook his head. "No, I don't. But that doesn't mean I don't understand the constant worry of being a parent. I'm thirty-one, and my mother still pampers me."

"I do not!" Alma gasped, outraged.

"Yes, you do." Andrew grinned, blowing his mother a kiss. "But I wouldn't have it any other way. Too used to it now, unfortunately."

Alma mumbled through her teeth about disobedient rascals as she stood up and filled the tray with new cups. After putting more warm buns in the basket, she took a deep, strengthening breath and left the two in the kitchen, joining her not-too-friendly friends upstairs again.

"I will never understand why she puts up with those hags." Andrew sighed, staring at the empty doorway. "They behave like she's some kind of servant, and she lets them. I've never heard her complain once."

"Everyone wants to fit in."

"I don't."

She smiled tenderly. "No, I guess not. You have never cared much about fitting in."

"Still don't, I'm afraid. My mother frets a lot about it, always has, but I can't help it if I don't see things the same way she does. I don't care if Sally Barnes thinks I'm a big clumsy clown, as long as I know I'm not."

Bathing in the warmth of his smile, Gillian relaxed. It was such a nice, familiar feeling, sitting with him at a kitchen table, chatting. Thirteen years had gone by since the last time, and yet, looking at his open, honest face, she could have sworn it was just the other day.

"It's so nice to see you again, Andy. It makes me realize how much I've missed you since I left Barnesville."

"You could have called."

His voice was soft, with a sad undertone, telling her how she must have turned his world upside down when she left. It had always been the two of them against the rest of the world, even though they had belonged to a larger gang of friends.

She closed her eyes, knowing he was right. She should have called. It wasn't as if she hadn't thought about it over the years, but something always seemed to get in the way. To be honest, when she first left Barnesville, alone and pregnant, she hadn't been able to think about anything but surviving.

But as the pieces of her life's puzzle started to fit together, thoughts about the people she had left behind started to pop up. She had wondered a lot about what had happened to them all, especially Andrew.

And Luke.

"You have to face him sometime." Again Andrew read her mind, and she wished she could rush away from him with some lame excuse, as she had the last time he mentioned the name she once had filled notepad after notepad with, each time surrounded by a heart.

"No, I don't."

"Come with me to Rosa's. It's Thursday, and everyone goes there for late luncheon, to meet and catch up. Even Luke."

Gillian shrank back. "No."

"You have to meet the gang sooner or later, so why not go now and have it over and done with?"

"I would prefer not to, thank you very much."

"They have asked about you."

Not knowing what to say, and too much in need of avoiding what felt like a fate worse than death, Gillian collected the dirty dishes and carried them over to the sink. Ignoring the dishwasher beside her, she filled the sink with hot water and started to carefully clean one of her mother's expensive cups.

"Don't you want to know what happened to your friends? We meant everything to you when you were a child, and now you can't even pretend you once cared?"

Water splashed out over the kitchen floor as Gillian dropped the delicate cup, ignoring the *crash* that followed.

"Of course I care," she howled at Andrew, who

leaned back in his chair, crossing his arms over his chest.

"You do? And yet you refuse to at least meet them and make sure they are all right. They care enough about you to ask me how you're doing, but you refuse to even mention them. As soon as I say their names you turn all pale and escape with your tail between your legs." All the warmth of Andrew's smile was gone as he glared at her angrily. "You know, when you left we all moved on with our lives. We had to. We hadn't the time to let the past set us back. Yet you, who were the one to leave, seem unable to let the past go."

"I care," she repeated, too humiliated over his truthful words to say anything else.

"Then come with me. Meet them. Eat lunch and then go. Forget us all again."

She sank back against the sink, the flaring anger gone as quickly as it had arrived. "I never forgot you all. I—I just was too busy with everything else. With Daisy…"

He stood and went to her, grabbing her soapy, wet hands in his. "I understand, Gilly. We all do. It's not as if it was so hard for us to find out where you had gone, to seek you out. But we didn't. Life kept going here, too."

She looked up at him, knowing she couldn't refuse him anything. He was her hero, her knight in shining armor. The one who had always been there for her when she was young, nursed her knees when bruised and her heart when she cried over her mother and Luke.

"Is he married?"

Andrew let go of her hands, grinning mischievously. "As a matter of fact, no. Lucas Walker

19

is as unmarried as he was the day you left."

"Did he ever open the car shop he talked about? The one in which he would dedicate his life to renovating all mistreated classic cars to their former splendor?"

Andrew shook his head. "No. He didn't. He joined the Marines and traveled to different danger spots all over the world, until one day he had enough and came back home to join another force."

"What other force?" She frowned as he sent her another dazzling smile.

"He's the new minister."

Visions of the young Luke, a restless rebel in the spirit of James Dean, flashed before her eyes. That he had joined the Marines fitted the image she had of him. Yet—a minister?

"But…Luke never believed in anything!"

"A decade in the armed forces made him find his faith in the good Lord. He's excelling on the post, a much adored shepherd for us all. Even the young ladies of the town now eagerly get up early in the morning every Sunday just to be able to sit in church, staring at him as much as they want as he gives the sermon."

"Still a looker, I guess?"

"Oh, yes. A ruggedly handsome former rebel, a Marine turned minister? How much more attractive can a man get?"

"Poor young girls."

"They never knew what hit them."

"Could you two cease this ruckus? Poor Rachel can't get her well-deserved rest when you two stand here in the kitchen shouting."

Sally Barnes hadn't changed much, Gillian

thought, as the older woman floated into the room. Her sharp eyes didn't miss any details, and at her disparaging look Gillian had never felt as wrinkly and in need of a shower before.

"Andrew Marshall, for being the town doctor, you sure aren't behaving with the dignity the post deserves. Your poor mother is so embarrassed upstairs."

"We're sorry, Sally." Andrew flashed his contagious smile, but this was a stone that wasn't easily touched. Sally barely quirked the corners of her tight lips, stretching them just enough to show a hint of a smile.

Bravely Andrew threw an arm around Gillian's waist, hauling her closer to him. "We were just leaving. Thursday luncheon, you know. Any message you wish us to deliver to your son when we meet him?"

"No."

"We'll be off then." Andrew moved toward the patio door, dragging the unwilling Gillian with him. "I'll have Gilly back before she's missed."

"She won't be."

Sally's words echoed inside Gillian's head as she climbed into Andrew's old, rusty truck and they drove the short distance toward Main Street. Of course she wouldn't be missed. She wasn't wanted here at all.

"I'm sorry." Andrew grimaced slightly. "You didn't deserve such impoliteness. Of course you would be missed. Rachel would notice immediately if you weren't in the house."

"No, she wouldn't."

"Gilly…"

She threw her hands up in despair. "I just don't get it. *Why* did she send for me? She definitely doesn't want me to be here. When I walked through the door that first day, she didn't even recognize me. I had to tell her who I was, and then she asked what I was doing here. As if I were a salesman, or someone else she couldn't wait to get rid of."

"She loves you."

"No, Andy, she doesn't. She's just not a loving person. It's not her fault, though. She was brought up by an uncaring widower who detested emotions or any show of frivolity. She just doesn't have any emotions inside her. I know. I have read her diaries from when she was young. Every last one of them contains only recollections of other people and their affairs, not her own. No feelings, no love, nothing. She hardly mentioned my father at all, or having any deeper emotions for him."

"It was an arranged marriage, we all know that, so what did you expect?"

"Something, I guess." She sighed. "Something giving away that she had felt something for anyone. All my life I've dreamt about her telling me how much she loves me. I—I think I just desperately hoped she once felt something for someone, because if she had, she might even...love me."

"*I* love you."

Hitting him lightly on the arm, Gillian laughed. "Of course you do. You have no choice. We made a pact of blood, remember?"

He wiggled his eyebrows at her. "I do remember. And I also remember we promised each other, with another bloody handshake, to share our first kiss together."

"We did, didn't we? Oh, my, what a couple we

were. Our poor parents. No wonder my mother looks at me with despair."

He parked the car outside the diner, but neither of them moved as they took in the laughing people inside the windows. It was amazing, Gillian thought. They hadn't changed a bit. They were older and more mature, but still…

Candice Lee stood by the table, a notepad in her hand, taking her friends' orders. She had worked at Rosa's Diner ever since she was thirteen and had been caught stealing from the register. She had her lovely mahogany hair in a bun on the top of her head, and the pink waitress dress she wore showed every last curve of her sexy body, just as it had back in Gillian's days of living in town.

Her sister, Megan Lee Barnes, was a year younger than the other girls but had still hung with their gang. She was the beautiful homecoming queen who had married the popular quarterback, just as she was supposed to do. Her high school boyfriend and now husband, Matthew Barnes, was the only child of Sally Barnes. He had been a coldhearted bully in school. Looking at his hard face and Megan's anxious one now, Gillian could tell not much had changed there.

And then there was Lucas Walker. Coming from one of the poorest families of Barnesville, from the wrong side of the Housatonic River, he'd had more attitude than money. Always in worn clothes inherited from some older cousin, he had fought his way through school. He was a year older than she, forced to go through second grade twice.

Her heart skipped a beat as she took in his tall frame and handsome face. Thirteen years had gone by, and he still looked the same. His dark hair was too long, hiding his intense brown eyes. He wore dark clothing that emphasized his lean body, showing he was still the heartthrob he had been all those years ago when most of the girls in school had been in love with him, including Gillian. The only thing that had changed since she'd seen him last was the clerical collar he wore. To her it looked as misplaced as a black sheep among white. But he seemed at ease with it, wearing it almost proudly.

As if he felt her gaze, Luke tensed slightly before looking directly at her through the window to where she sat in Andrew's truck. His dark eyes took in what he saw, and the small, crooked smile she remembered so well grew on his lips. A tingling sensation started to build inside her, and she took a deep, staggering breath.

"Are you ready?"

Andrew's soft voice broke through her dazed thoughts, and with more confidence than she felt she nodded. "Yes, I am."

With Andrew's supportive arm around her waist, she walked through the door, feeling more excitement than she had in years. Could this be what she needed, a reunion with her past? Maybe her old friends would help her get over all her bad memories and help her move on with her life.

And as Luke came forward to greet her, his dark hair glistening in the cold light from the fluorescent lamp, she couldn't stop herself from thinking that maybe she would be able to give Daisy what she wished for the most—a father.

Chapter Three

"I can hardly believe it's been thirteen years already. It feels like it was only yesterday we ran down to Oak Lane and stole apples from Mr. Busby's garden."

Ignoring her boss's obvious irritation over her lack of interest for other customers, Candice gracefully sat down beside Gillian in the same booth they'd spent too many hours in during their childhood and teen years.

"Just because nothing's changed in your life, Candy, doesn't mean the clock doesn't continue ticking for the rest of us." Matthew leaned back with an overbearing smile, his blue eyes clear of emotion. "It must be so embarrassing for you that your life is the same as it was when Gillian left. Heck, you still wear the same clothes as you did then."

Disrespectfully, Candice stuck her tongue out at her brother-in-law before turning back to Gillian with an apologizing shrug. "Don't mind him. He's still upset over me not wanting to have anything to do with him back then. He's just not man enough to handle rejection."

"I'm all the man you'd ever need, sweetheart."

The men laughed at Matthew's masculine joke, but his wife hissed, "Matt, that's too much, even for you," effectively ending the manly hoots of laughter.

Awkwardly, the other two men mumbled their

apologies, but not Matthew. With a sneer he leaned toward Megan, his cold gaze not leaving the fragile beauty of her face. "Is there something bugging you, sweetheart?"

She shrank back, mumbling something inaudible that rendered her another husbandly sneer.

"I thought so."

Nobody said anything for a few moments, an uncomfortable silence hovering over the booth and its six occupants.

Matthew leaned back again, crossing his arms over his chest. Gillian wanted nothing so much as to wipe the supercilious smile off his face, but she restrained herself. This was not her fight. Not yet, at least. She had just returned and didn't know what lay behind it. As no one else stepped in—not even the cocky Candice—she knew there had to be more to the story than what met the eye.

Matthew had always been a bully, but in an overbearing and cocky way—never downright mean. Gillian had never liked him; he was too brutish and direct, and he didn't listen to anyone else's thoughts, as tactful and intuitive as a steamroller.

Megan had been his girlfriend since junior high, always there at his beck and call. Gillian had never understood what she saw in him, this big, brawny guy who always wanted to be in the middle of everyone's attention.

"It's like he's put a spell on her, turned her into a human puppet," Candice had sighed once when they were dissecting the strange relationship between her sister and her overbearing boyfriend. Gillian couldn't have agreed more. Megan seemed spineless and without a will of her own when it came to the man in her life.

And now she was caught. Trapped in the everyday life of a stay-at-home mom, with no education and with no interests but her dictatorial husband's wellbeing and the lives of their children.

"Are you back for good, or is it just a temporary visit?" Megan asked Gillian politely, breaking through the wall of tension Matthew's harshness had built.

"It's temporary, for my mother's sake only. We will go back home in a couple of weeks, when the next semester starts for Daisy."

"That's too bad." Megan seemed genuinely disappointed. "I would have loved for you to come back to Barnesville for good, the whole gang together again."

"We have an excellent school here too," Matthew chimed in, his earlier contempt gone now when he could act as the mayor, promoting the town he singlehandedly commanded. "I'm sure your daughter would fit right in."

"Thank God Mrs. Cooper quit last year." Andrew grinned mischievously. "Otherwise Daisy would have had to endure her, just as we once had to."

Gillian choked on the water she was drinking.

"Was Mrs. Cooper still teaching last year? She was more or less dying when we went to junior high twenty years ago. I would have thought she was gone way before now."

"She's a tough old bird." Matthew sounded almost impressed. "It didn't matter what we did or said, she refused to give notice until she was ready to leave. And now she's pestering poor Luke here, instead, organizing both him and the church."

"What can I say? She adores me."

Luke's crooked smile made Gillian lightheaded. Oh, how she had loved that slow smile of his when she was younger. It was such a wonderful smile, starting deep inside his brown eyes, slowly growing warmer and warmer until it reached his mouth, dragging one corner of his mouth upwards.

"She certainly acts like a watchdog for the poor man." Matthew laughed heartily over his own joke. "She's not letting anyone come closer to him than a mile, especially females. Poor old Luke, he will live his life like a monk and die a lonely man in the wrinkly arms of his benefactress."

At first Luke seemed almost irritated, as if Matthew had unknowingly succeeded in striking a very tender chord. But then his crooked smile returned in full force. "Lucky for me, then, she can't be with me twenty-four seven. If she only knew what's going on in my rooms when she's not around…"

"Oh, sweet Lord, have mercy! Don't tell the woman about your orgies. She would sell that little house of hers and move in with you to guard your chastity with her life."

"Can you imagine living with Mrs. Cooper?" Candice shuddered. "Every day you would have to listen to her lecturing you about the right way to open a door, peel potatoes, or whatever else you possibly could do in the wrong way."

"I can imagine it could stress one's patience endlessly," Andrew said diplomatically, and they all laughed lightly.

"Oh, Andrew." Candice put her arms around him, pressing her curvaceous body close to his. "Promise me you'll never change, you sweet, adorable man."

"Oh, for heaven's sake, Candice!" Matthew snorted, rolling his eyes almost too dramatically. "Take your hands off the poor doctor. He deserves better than to have you all over him. Go plaster yourself on someone else. I'm sure there must be at least one customer in here you haven't had in your bed yet."

Again an awkward silence spread, and Gillian looked at the stern faces surrounding her. So much had happened during the last thirteen years, and it suddenly dawned upon her that these five people were not her friends anymore.

They were now strangers who just happened to be people she once had known. Distant acquaintances she could talk with for a couple of hours about joint memories but then had nothing in common with as soon as they left the past and moved into the present.

But then again…

Somehow they all still were the same as they had been all those years ago. Matthew was the loud bully who almost compulsively had to say his bad, belittling jokes. Megan, who never had had a will of her own, still stared silently at Matthew, awaiting his instructions about what to say, what to think, what to do.

The generous Candice with her warm heart and voluptuous body still had trouble saying no, and men with larger needs than consciences took advantage of her unselfishness. Andrew was, as always, the caretaker, the one person everyone turned to in their hour of need, but no one ever asked or cared about how he was doing.

And then there was Luke.

She had to admit he had changed. A lot. When she left he had been the town bad boy. A rebel without a cause. But he had changed his direction in life and surprised them all with his newfound faith and love for God and humanity.

But then again… As she looked into his eyes she still could see the same restlessness and feeling of inferiority he had suffered from in their youth.

Maybe it was she who had changed. Maybe it was she who didn't fit in anymore. Had her years away from Barnesville made her find who she truly was and made her able to escape from the box she once had been in?

As the meal progressed, she found herself sinking back, becoming an observer instead of a participant. Her friends continued their bickering, always holding themselves inside the box they'd been in for years, not once trying to leave their place and be something else.

What small, square lives they led.

Her mother might have, unbeknownst, given her the best gift Gillian ever could get—a way to find herself and her own strengths.

She was so lost in her thoughts that she at first didn't notice the others starting to leave. Not until a hand covered hers did she wake up and met Luke's brown eyes.

"What planet were you on?" he joked, and she felt her heart skip a beat.

"I'm so sorry. My thoughts wandered off…" She looked around the table, noticing the others collecting their things, putting money on the table. Candice had already left them, openly flirting with the men at the table next to them as she took their orders.

"Do you have somewhere you must go, or is it possible for you to come with me? I have some things at the church for Rachel. The people in the community have left gifts for her, food and supplies, mostly, but also memorabilia for her to remember them by before she leaves this life."

Feeling her cheeks growing warm, Gillian knew she blushed, and she quickly bent her head, pretending to search for her purse.

"Of course," she mumbled as she put some money on the table, making sure to tip Candice generously. "Let me just visit the ladies' room, and then I can go with you."

As she tried to walk past him, he grabbed her arm lightly, and she stopped. Reluctantly she lifted her head and met his dark gaze. He smiled at her, a small, crooked, secretive smile that made her toes curl with anticipation.

"Gillian Crane," he breathed, "if you only knew how happy I am to see you again."

She felt her lips part, and almost unwillingly his eyes moved downwards, growing darker as he took in her inviting mouth.

"Thirteen years have passed, and yet you two act as if you're still in high school."

Bewildered, Gillian ripped her eyes from Luke's and blushed again as Matthew stalked up to them, with Megan and Andrew close behind. Hesitantly Luke took a step back, to her relief putting some distance between the two of them.

With a forced laugh, Candice pushed her way through, reaching for the money on the table they had just left. "I hope you all tipped me accordingly. I have seen the most wonderful dress I just have to buy. It's quite costly, especially when one considers how little fabric it's made of."

Thankful for the diversion, Gillian slunk away to the ladies' room. She filled her hands with water, splashing the coldness all over her face in a desperate attempt to get rid of the telling blush.

What was wrong with her? Why couldn't she be as blasé as usual? At her work in New York, she was known as the Ice Queen—the one woman who didn't let her emotions guide her actions.

But as soon as she met Luke again all her hard-earned self-confidence had washed off and the geeky little girl emerged, too insecure to know how to handle the bristling emotions filling her.

"Are you all right?"

Megan came up behind her, and Gillian looked at her old friend in the stained mirror over the basin. "I'm just fine, thank you for asking."

"I—I don't w-want to pry, b-but you seemed a b-bit flustered, and I j-just wanted to make sure nothing M-Matthew said..." Her voice trailed off as another customer came into the room, and not until they were alone again did she continue. "Sometimes he seems t-to make p-people uncomfortable."

"Really, I'm fine." Gillian dried her hands before turning to face Megan. "Matthew didn't offend me in any way, I assure you."

"Are you sure?" Megan's relief seemed endless, and Gillian shook her head, unable to hold back a frown.

"How about you, Megan, are you all right?"

Her head bobbing up and down, Megan smiled radiantly. "I'm perfectly happy. Couldn't be better. I'm a mother too, you know. We have three beautiful girls who mean everything to me. I'm so blessed."

The last came almost as an afterthought, as if she tried to tell herself that she really was just that, blessed.

"Three girls?" Gillian forced a light laugh to sound as if nothing out of the ordinary had happened to her and meeting them all again after thirteen years didn't bother her at all. "My, my. How do you cope? I have only one, and she drives me crazy with her antics."

Megan laughed too, and this time it came from the heart, not forced at all. Her beautiful face shone radiantly as the love she felt for her children overcame her submissiveness. "I never said they didn't drive me crazy, did I? Oh, they are a bunch of monsters, but at the end of the day they are *my* monsters, and I wouldn't have them any other way."

"Tell me about it. It doesn't matter how many strange things Daisy does, I still love her so much it scares me."

"Megan!"

Wincing slightly, Megan paled as Matthew's bellow reached them from outside the restroom. With a quickly mumbled excuse, she rushed out the door, back into the diner, and Gillian followed her slowly.

"What took you so long? You said you just had to wash your hands, or was that just something you said so no one would know you needed to take a dump?"

Megan squirmed uncomfortably as Matthew hollered with laughter over his own distasteful joke. As the couple left the diner, Gillian couldn't help but feel sorry for Megan. She seemed crushed under her husband's heavy thumb, without the means or will to find her own way through life.

"Shall we go?" Always the gentleman, Andrew held open the door for her, assuming she was to join him in his truck.

"You'll have to go by yourself this time, Andy my man," Luke said as he walked up to Gillian and put his arm around her waist, the warmth of his hand against her hip. "Gillian and I are going to the church, where some things have been collecting for Rachel."

"People are sensing that her time is ending, I guess." Andrew's compassion washed over them. "Do you need two extra hands to help you?"

Luke shook his head. "No, we'll manage. But thanks. I appreciate the offer."

"Are you sure?"

"Go home, Andy." Luke laughed. "Sit down on that new sofa of yours you never use, pop a beer, and cuddle with Wifey. You have a few precious hours off, for once. Don't throw them away on Gillian and me."

"When you put it like that..." With a wink, Andrew strolled back toward his truck, whistling a happy little tune.

"That man doesn't know what it means to rest," Luke said as they watched the doctor's truck drive away. "He's the most unselfish man I know, never turning anyone down when they ask for his help, no matter how small and insignificant their plight might seem."

"Even as a child he was generous, almost stupidly so," Gillian admitted. "He always prioritized everyone else's needs first, never his own. I don't know how many times he helped me with my homework and then had to rush with his own, barely able to finish in time. But it didn't matter what I said, he refused to do his first. In his world, mine was so much more important. Such unselfishness amazes me."

"That's the Andrew Marshall we all adore. A modern version of a knight in shining armor."

"Rather a knight in an old, rusty truck, I would say."

"That truck…" Luke shook his head as they walked out into the parking lot. "It will be the death of him, I'm sure. We all have tried to get him to buy another one, something safer, with four-wheel-drive, made for traveling out into the country, but he refuses. He insists his old one suits him just fine. Matthew, who is the most tightfisted mayor there ever was, even said the community could sponsor a new one for him. But no, Andrew still refused, told Matthew to give the money to people who really needed it."

"Even though the doctor refuses to buy a new vehicle, it seems the minister doesn't mind one," Gillian teased as they reached Luke's modern muscle car. According to the commercials Gillian had seen, it had more horsepower than anyone ever could use on the small roads surrounding Barnesville.

Luke's eyes glistened under the curtain of thick brown hair, but he didn't answer her tease. Instead he helped her into the car before seating himself and firing up the engine, and they left the diner and drove down Main Street under the heavy oak trees.

She didn't know if it was just her, but the tension in the air felt thick enough to carve into pieces, almost unbearable in the small compartment of the car.

"So, how is Rachel?" he asked.

"Not good. Her heart has given up, and now we all just wait for it to stop completely. Andrew says it will be any day now."

"I'm sorry."

Tears at his compassion filled her eyes, and she hid her face from him, staring unseeingly through the window at her side. As if he could sense her need of solitude, he remained silent. It was not until they reached the church that he talked to her again.

"Here it is, the church I used to stay as far away from as possible and that now means everything to me."

Gillian looked up at the tall building, admiring the beautiful craftsmanship. "I've always thought this had to be one of the most beautiful churches there was, and now since I've seen more of the world than just Barnesville, I still feel the same. It's glorious."

He walked up the few steps to the large double door, where he turned and held out his hand to her.

"Come," he said, his intense brown eyes mesmerizing her. "Come into my kingdom."

Almost as if in a trance she moved up the stairs and put her trembling hand in his. As they walked into the church, a sensational feeling of serenity filled her heart and soul, and in that moment she knew she had made the right choice when she decided to return to Barnesville. Looking at the man who led her down the aisle, she knew nothing had changed over the years.

Luke Walker still made her heart flutter.

Chapter Four

"Why on earth did someone think my mother needed an old fryer in her last couple of days?" Gillian giggled as she held up the stained appliance no one in their right mind ever would use for cooking something they intended to eat.

Luke looked up from the bag in which he had packed some of the things Gillian was going to take home with her, his eyes glistening in the light from the chandelier over his head. "It's the thought that counts, Gillian, and besides, I just couldn't tell the man who donated it I found it unnecessary, especially not after he assured me this machine made the best darn fries this side of the Hudson River."

"I wouldn't know what to do with it. Mother already has one and, as far as I know, almost never uses it."

"Why don't you leave it here, then, together with anything else you can spare, and I will make sure it finds its way to someone who will appreciate it."

Relieved, she put the fryer back on the table, and soon she had created a large pile of things she thought would be better left for someone other than her dying mother.

"Look at this," Luke called out to her, catching her attention. "Here's the old yearbook from our senior year. I haven't seen one of these since I got mine all those years ago."

Gillian sat down beside him, looking at the clean faces gazing up at her from the pages. She couldn't believe how young they all looked. She had thought herself an adult, ready to burst out into the world. But seeing her own small pictured face made her realize what a child she'd still been. She didn't look a day older than Daisy, who was twelve.

"Dear Lord, what did I do to my hair?"

Luke's laughter interrupted her sentimental thoughts, and she followed his finger to the little square with his name under.

He hadn't changed much.

What a heartthrob he had been, with those brown eyes squinting from under his dark windblown hair. Always in jeans and a worn leather jacket, he had been in a league of his own.

"You looked like James Dean," she said with a tender smile, and he laughed again.

"If you had told me that back then, I would have loved you forever. James Dean was my guiding star, you know, and I was desperately trying to do everything he had done—except dying young, that is."

"A rebel."

"No, not really. I hadn't the stamina. Looking back now, I must admit I was really pathetic. Thank God I joined the Marines, because that really put a spine in my back."

"I didn't find you the least pathetic," she said fondly, touching his picture with a light finger.

"I know you didn't. You and most of the girls found me utterly cool, something I unfortunately was a little too aware of."

"I was so in love with you."

"I know."

He smiled crookedly at her as she looked at him with surprise. "You were an open book back then, Gillian. Your sweet face always told the truth, and I knew you fancied me. Everyone knew."

"Why didn't you do anything about it, then, if you knew how I felt about you? It's not as if I would have denied you anything."

"You weren't that easy to get close to, Gillian. Whenever I tried to talk to you, you blushed fiercely before leaving me as soon as you could. I was too cool back then to follow one girl when there was so many in line. I was a heartless rascal."

He made himself sound like an awful person, as if he hadn't cared for anything or anyone. But that was not how she remembered him.

"You could have had me at your beck and call whenever you liked, but you didn't. That's not something a heartless rascal does."

"I probably would have, if it weren't for your mother and Andy."

Gillian leaned back so she could look into his eyes. "Andy? How does he have anything to do with you not wanting me?"

"He loved you."

"I know he did. We were best friends."

Luke grinned, looking more handsome than ever.

"He didn't love you as a friend, Gillian. He loved you with all his heart, and out of respect to him I just couldn't bring myself to flirt with you. I might have if I had felt strongly about you, but I didn't. In my eyes, you were Andy's girl, and that made you untouchable."

"I wasn't Andy's girl."

"Yes, you were," he said compassionately. "We all knew you were. That is, everyone except you. Poor Andy. He loved you so much back then, and you never saw him as anything but a friend."

"Now you make me feel awful."

He laughed loudly over her stunned admission. "Don't. Just as it's not my fault I never made a move on you, it is not your fault he never told you how he truly felt. But, to be completely honest, I did regret I never did anything about you, after you left. Not that I think it would have meant anything in the long run, though. I wasn't an emotional man back then, and I wouldn't have stayed with you. In the end, I must say I think it worked out quite well as it did. You found a new life in the city, and I found my true calling in the midst of the horrors of war."

Gillian didn't listen to him, too lost in her scattered thoughts. "He never said a word. During all those years we were friends, he never once hinted about feeling something more for me than pure friendship."

"Would you have listened to him if he had?"

She shook her head with a wry laugh. "Probably not. I was too caught up in yearning for you. I was a teenage girl, after all, and they do tend to dwell a bit."

"A bit?"

It felt so good, laughing together. Her heart fluttered as he looked at her with his intense brown eyes, just as it had thirteen years ago. She still dwelled, she realized, looking back down on the yearbook, meeting her own innocent gaze.

"I can go with you, if you like."

Dazed, she looked at him, unable to follow his train

of thought. "Excuse me?"

"It's almost dinner time. How about you and I take a bag each, and I'll walk you home."

"Such a gentleman."

"Comes with the collar. I just can't help myself nowadays. It seems I just have to help and forgive. Quite annoying sometimes, I assure you."

"How irritating."

"It is. There's nothing better than to hold on to a grudge, no matter how small it is, nursing it properly for a while. Grudges do age well, you know."

"And they say women dwell."

"We men don't dwell. We just…linger a bit. Discuss it at our local shack over a beer or two—but *then* we let it go."

His arm brushed against hers as he stood up and silently ushered her to follow him outside. With a sense of sacredness, she put her hand on the throbbing spot on her arm, feeling as though touched by an angel. He stopped at the door, beckoning her to follow, and breathlessly she stood up and grabbed the bags.

It was a beautiful evening outside, warm and inviting. The fragile, flowery scent of summer filled the air, deliciously mixed with the intoxicating aroma from dozens of barbecues. Farther down the street someone turned on a radio playing happy tunes from the fifties, and as the sun started to set, the golden sunbeams turned the quiet small-town street into a shiny yellow brick road.

It was magical, and Gillian could hardly breathe as she took in the scenery. It was as if all things in nature worked together to create the perfect setting for her walk with Luke, to make it into something so fulfilling neither of them could withstand the sultry promise of the night.

She felt his gaze upon her as they slowly walked down the street, and all her old insecurity came back. Did he like what he saw? She had never been a smashing beauty, but over the years she had learned how to make the best of what she had.

"You look great," he said, as if he had read her mind and wanted to assure her he did indeed like what he saw.

"Thank you." She had never been more appreciative of twilight's dimness as it blurred his vision enough to hide the telltale blush discoloring her cheeks.

"Are you seeing someone back home?"

"No."

"Well, that's wonderful news."

His grin was filled with promises, and she felt a childish need to ask him to pinch her arm hard, so she would know for sure this was not just one of her romantic childhood daydreams.

Slowly, as if he didn't want to scare her, he moved closer to her so they walked shoulder to shoulder. He shifted the bag he carried to his other side before taking her hand, holding it steadily as they continued down the street.

She definitely felt like a teenager again.

It was as if the last thirteen years had flown away and she again had only one mission—to become Mrs. Lucas Walker. When she was younger she would have given her life for a chance to live through what she did just now, walking with Luke hand in hand.

But she wasn't that girl anymore. Adulthood and

surviving the obstacles of life had taught her to not believe in the impossible. She had learned the hard way to trust what she knew she had. Yet as she sneaked a peek at his handsome profile, something inside told her to let go, to let loose and start living life.

"Here we are." Luke's soft voice broke through her wandering thoughts, and she looked up at the hovering façade of her childhood home. Darkness and silence met her gaze. Not a person could be seen through the large bay windows facing the street.

"It looks like all the ladies have left for today. The house is too peaceful for them to still be around." She sighed, relieved, and he grinned again, that wonderful crooked smile of his.

"I know most of them from church, and I can imagine they are quite a handful for you to cope with. They are not known for their subtlety and common sense, and I feel for you, having to put up with them while trying to live through your mother's last days on this earth."

"You have a wonderful way with words, Pastor Walker. I bet you rock those sermons of yours."

"Why don't you come and see—or hear—for yourself this Sunday?" His brown eyes sparkled with mirth. "I promise you will encounter something you've never seen or heard before."

"Oh, I can only guess," she teased back. "I've heard all about the first rows being filled to the brim with starry-eyed girls, all desperately in love with the handsome clergyman."

His deep laughter echoed in the darkness of the evening, and reluctantly she let go of his hand and climbed the short stair until she stood on the porch. As she turned to gaze back down at him, she tried to look as indifferent as her pounding heart would allow. "Would you perhaps like a cup of coffee before you go?"

She met his brown eyes, almost drowning in their intensity, as he slowly made his way up the steps until he stood beside her on the porch.

"To be honest," he said softly with his dark, smooth voice, "I think a cup of coffee with you would be absolutely divine."

The radio down the street changed tunes, and the soft tones of an old love song traveled through the still air, embracing them. Slowly, as if he didn't want to frighten her, Luke bent his head, and she forgot how to breathe as his lips closed in on hers.

This was what she had wished for her whole life— Lucas Walker kissing her—and for a moment she felt almost panicky, afraid that now, when it finally happened, she would be disappointed.

As she felt his breath against her face, she closed her eyes, feeling like a teenager as she waited for his lips to finally touch hers.

"Oops! I didn't know someone was out here."

They flew apart as Andrew's surprised voice broke through the intense silence on the porch. Luke drew a hand through his hair, looking as embarrassed as Gillian felt.

"No worries, Andy."

"Are you sure?" Andrew grinned mischievously. "If I had been in your shoes I wouldn't have liked being interrupted."

Luke made a small uncomfortable grimace. "I was just seeing Gillian home, helping her with the bags..."

"You don't have to excuse yourself to me, Luke," Andrew interrupted kindly. "You are both adults and without strings. It was bound to happen, I guess."

"It's just that…" Luke seemed unable to find the right words, and Andrew put a calming hand on his arm.

"Don't fret, Luke, I won't tell. But I have to warn you—you know what they are like, the Barnesville Hyenas. Without mercy. They will shred you into pieces if they find out you have been frolicking, and outside in clear view of anyone who wanted to watch. And they would not stop with you. They would go after Gillian, too. I fear she would suffer quite badly before the Hyenas were finished tearing her life and respectability apart."

"You give them more power than they have—or deserve. I know they would be very upset with me if I did something improper, but to completely destroy both my life and Gillian's because of it? No, I don't think so. But I hear you…"

Andrew didn't answer, but Gillian could tell he disagreed with Luke. If anyone knew what the women of Barnesville were like, it was he. All his life he had borne the surveillance of their callous eyes that never missed anything. They knew everything there was to know about him, and Gillian could only guess it was his warm, caring heart and kind, compassionate personality that had made them accept him as their new doctor and confidant when old Doc Brown passed away.

"Well." With another little grimace, Luke moved reluctantly toward the steps. "It's time for me to go. Dinner's about to be served in the boarding house."

She didn't mind he was leaving, which surprised

her a bit. She would have thought Andrew interrupting them and now Luke leaving would annoy her, but it didn't. She felt almost relieved. It was too much too soon.

It was one thing to live in Barnesville and yearn for Luke every day and never be kissed. It was a whole other thing to meet him again after thirteen years and almost kiss him the same day.

The truth was she didn't know him anymore.

Heck, she had hardly known him thirteen years earlier, either, considering what he had told her about how he had seen things back then. She had made him into someone special, someone outstanding, but the truth was that he had been just a normal teenage boy, with just as much insight as a dishrag.

As Luke disappeared down the road, she sneaked a peek at Andrew, who stood beside her, staring thoughtfully out into the front garden.

So he had been in love with her.

That was definitely one of the biggest surprises of her life. If it was true, she would never have known about it if Luke hadn't told her. Andrew had never said anything about feeling more for her than sister-of-heart and best friend. They had spent hours upon hours alone, talking about nothing and everything, so it wasn't as if he hadn't had a chance to say something.

Although… Her favorite subject had been Luke, talking endlessly about him and how fantastic he was. If Andrew had wanted to say something to her, she had not made it easy for him to open up.

"What?"

She looked into his kind eyes smiling inquiringly toward her as he caught her staring at him, and a wave of gratefulness washed over her. Thank God he never had told her about his feelings for her back then. She would not have handled that situation well at all, if he had.

The truth was she would probably have hurt him quite harshly if she had been told. She had not been an insightful person back then either.

Teenagers usually weren't.

"Nothing." She shrugged awkwardly, trying to seem indifferent, but when he frowned she knew she hadn't succeeded. Luckily for her, Andrew had never been one to pry, and he immediately let the subject go.

"What a beautiful afternoon," he said instead, changing the subject to something much more neutral.

"Fantastic."

"Do you hear the birds? It's like there's a whole chorus of them, with an orchestra of crickets and bees, playing accompaniment to that radio."

"Amazing."

They stood silent for a while, looking out into the garden, listening to the soft twitters and other sounds, and Gillian relaxed a bit. It had been an overly eventful day, one that had gotten her more uptight than she liked.

Standing in the soft light of the porch, side by side with Andrew, soothed her. He never craved anything from her, never expected her to be something she wasn't. That was an unusual feeling for her. Most people in her life wanted something from her.

"So, you and Luke, then?"

"Uh-hum."

"I didn't know you two were out here on the porch. I would never have barged out, if I had. I didn't mean to interrupt."

"It's all right, Andrew, really it is. I'm kind of glad you did. I don't think I was ready to kiss him, not just yet anyway. It has dawned on me I hardly know the man. He's a completely different person now, and the Luke I was bent on kissing was the teenager he was the last time I saw him."

"Then I am glad I did interrupt."

They laughed together, and he put his arm around her, hauling her closer to him. Naturally, just as she had when they were young, she put her arms around his waist and buried her nose in his shirt.

He still smelled of cookies and dry earth, just as he had when they were young. It was a familiar and intoxicating smell, and for a small moment, as she stood there in his safe arms with her ear pressed against his heart, she felt sad over the fact that he was married.

She felt him rest his chin against the top of her head, and she knew this was what she wanted. Not Andrew—he was unavailable anyway—but the safe zone he offered her without any ulterior motive.

And not only for herself, but for Daisy, too. No wonder Daisy was fixated at the thought of finding out who her father really was. She had never experienced something like this, a man's strong embrace. Gillian had never known her father either, but she'd had Andrew. And even though the boy she had known was far from the man who held her now, he still had made her feel at ease and worry-free.

But how would she ever be able to give her daughter a father's love, when all Daisy wanted was her biological father?

And finding him was something Gillian couldn't

help her with. The utterly humiliating truth was that Gillian didn't know who Daisy's father was.

Chapter Five

"Your mother asked for you."

Gillian sighed and let go of Andy's waist, ending the embrace. When he removed his arms, she shivered as the air's coolness reached her, and she followed him into the house, into the warmth.

"How is she?"

"Not good, I'm afraid. She hasn't got many days left now, maybe just hours. Her heart is failing her, and soon it will stop."

She nodded, feeling smaller and smaller by the minute. She had never had a good relationship with her mother, had always been pushed away, but she still loved Rachel Crane. Nothing could change that, and the mere thought of losing the only parent she had left scared her immensely.

"Shall we?"

She followed him up the grand stairs and entered her mother's bedroom, which now was desolate and quiet since all the visitors had gone. Her mother lay still in her bed, her eyes closed tightly.

For a second Gillian thought she had already died. Panic made her weak, and she staggered into a pedestal standing just inside the door.

"For goodness' sake, child! Can't you even walk into a room without bumping into something?" Rachel's sharp voice cut through the dense air, and

Gillian mumbled an excuse, too relieved to be annoyed at her mother's rudeness.

"Rachel, you're awake," Andrew said cheerfully as he lit the light on her nightstand.

"Turn that off."

Ignoring Rachel's irritated retort, Andrew reached for Rachel's hand to feel her pulse. "How are you feeling, Rachel? Your heart beats too fast; you need to calm down. We don't want you to get too tired, do we now?"

The look Rachel gave him would have subdued other men into a pile of nothing, but not Andrew. He only smirked, ignoring her frustration with him.

"Gillian's back from the church."

"I noticed. I hope my pedestal didn't get nicked. It means a lot to me."

Gillian shook her head, eager to please her mother in any way she could, now when she knew their days together were coming to an end. "No, Mother, it looks just fine. I can't see any damage."

"Andrew," Rachel ordered. "Can you see for yourself if what Gillian says is the truth? Considering she is the one who stumbled into it, I don't trust her opinion about my pedestal's wellbeing."

"Oh, come on," Andrew soothed Rachel, when he noticed Gillian's expression at her mother's nasty remark. "That pedestal isn't important. Gillian is. Why don't you two seize the moment and have a nice chat, just the two of you, now that all the hyenas have left the building."

What a wonderful idea. The irritation she'd felt vanished, and Gillian turned toward her mother with an inviting smile. Rachel wasn't as obliging, though.

"How can you suggest I should throw away the few precious days I have left, just to talk with Gillian? I think I have said enough to her through the years. No, I don't need that now. I need peace and quiet."

"But Mother…"

Rachel closed her eyes, pointedly ending the one-sided conversation. "You can go now."

"Mother!"

"Gillian, please. For once in your life, can't you just humor me? I don't want you here now. Go away and leave me alone."

Tears pricked Gillian's eyes as she looked down on her mother's stern face. Not even when dying would Rachel Crane give in to love and her daughter's need to be near her. She wouldn't give Gillian the chance to ask the questions burning inside her or even let her say goodbye.

With a whimper, Gillian ran out through the bedroom door, only to barge straight into Sally Barnes, who had been standing just outside the door, listening.

"Watch your step," she said icily, but Gillian was too upset to care.

It couldn't be much clearer. Her mother didn't want her around. Why had the woman sent for her? To amuse herself coming up with ten new ways to turn her daughter into a nervous, unwanted, blubbering mess?

She dived into the living room and sat on one of the sofas, hiding her crying face in her hands. She heard Andrew's heavy steps as he joined her, but she hadn't the strength to ask him to go away.

She wasn't her mother. She needed someone.

When he settled beside her, she threw herself into his arms and, for the first time since her return, let go of all restraints. Sobs tore through her as she cried for what could have been, for what should have been, and for the pain her mother's indifference inflicted.

"There, there," Andrew mumbled, gently stroking her back, and she tightened her grip on him, pressing her body close to his almost as if she wanted to get inside him to find a hiding place where no one ever would find her.

"I hate her." She sniffed as the sobbing started to calm down, and she felt his breath against her forehead as he looked down on her.

"No, you don't."

"Yes, I do. I hate her so much I ache with the need to hurt her as badly as she's hurt me. To see the pain I feel in my heart echo in her eyes."

"That's not hate, that's disappointment. I thought you knew by now your mother is who she is. Don't expect more from her than she's able to give you."

"She's my mother. Loving me shouldn't be something this hard for her, should it?"

"It's not always so easy to just *love*."

Lifting her head she met his warm, compassionate gaze. "Are you telling me I'm not a lovable person, in a strange backwards effort to comfort me?"

He threw his head back as his hearty laughter filled the air. "My God, Gillian, you never give up, do you? Of course you are lovable. No one who meets you can help but love you. What I tried to say is that sometimes it's not enough with just one person loving another. Love *is* strange, as you know, and to be completely honest, it doesn't last forever—it *can* falter if not returned. In Rachel's case, she's got too much baggage emotionally to show you she does care. You have to consider the fact that you have been away for thirteen years, Gillian. That's a long, long time."

"So you mean the reason for her not loving me is that I've been away from her all these years?"

Andrew sighed, frustrated, for once losing his usual casual air. "Gilly, you have to stop this strange fixation with what your mother feels for you. Or rather what your mother *doesn't* feel for you. My meaning was that maybe she's just got too used to appearing indifferent toward you and Daisy in front of everyone else, so that she doesn't know how to show the two of you how much she *does* care, now when you both are here."

"You are not making any sense at all."

"I'm a man; I'm not supposed to."

"That's one weak excuse."

Again his amused laughter filled the room, and again she leaned back against him, tucking her head under his chin. She closed her eyes as his arms tightened around her.

Why had she never before realized what a perfect man Andrew Marshall was? Not until now, when it was too late—he was already married and, as it unfortunately seemed, happily so—did she finally appreciate just how special he was. As he placed a chaste kiss on her forehead, her whole body tingled, and the heat building inside her had her almost breathless.

With a reluctant sigh, he lifted her off his lap and got to his feet. "I'm so sorry, Gilly, but I have to go. I've promised a patient of mine to come by before nightfall, so I must leave now before it's too late."

She stood too, silently watching him gather his things. He looked the essence of a country doctor in his practical pants and knitted sweater. It was just the golf clubs missing to fulfill the image.

Catching her staring at him, he sent her another warm smile, and she had to sit down again as wave upon wave of a destructive need to kiss him took over her whole being.

It was amazing. Without even trying, Andrew had wakened a part of her she hadn't known she possessed—a woman's need to be near a man. She had learned the hard way to take care of herself and Daisy by hardening her heart toward everyone else in order to focus on putting their daily bread on the table. It was no wonder they called her the Ice Queen at work. She had always refused to let go of her control, preferring to spend what free time she had with her daughter and then on any second job she could do from home during the dark hours of night when Daisy slept.

The few dates she'd managed to drag herself off to had been complete disasters. The men had mostly been interested in sex or an occasional relationship. Even though the latter should have been perfect for her current situation as a single mom with a career, she still couldn't do it.

She was a small-town girl at heart, and just the thought of having a steady relationship that wasn't meant to become anything more than sex…

Well, that just wouldn't do.

Loving Daisy had been enough for a long time, and she had pushed her womanly needs aside without any problem. At least until she returned to Barnesville and met Andrew and Luke again, which had now turned her life upside down.

Especially meeting Andrew.

The very married Andrew.

She could never let herself get between a man and his wife; she had too much respect for the love between two people and for the commitment they'd made. But it was hard, she had to admit, as years of slumbering feelings overwhelmed her with euphoria.

It might be an old cliché, but she *did* feel like a volcano ready to erupt. And all because of a man she had never thought of as anything but a friend.

Luke's face popped up in her mind's eye, and she chewed thoughtfully on her lower lip. Her shallow heart reacted to him too, and she didn't know if it was because of old habit or because she was attracted to the man he was today. Would it be wrong of her to go to him to find out? She ransacked her heart, and the answer was a loud *no*. Of course it wouldn't. They were both single, with no obligations to anyone else, other than Daisy.

Andrew was a dead end, but Luke might be the open door to a new life for her. A part of her had never stopped loving him, and he had made it quite clear he was attracted to her. Maybe she could turn a teenager's fanatic infatuation into a woman's love?

"Could you drop me off at Luke's?" she asked Andrew, and his light smile disappeared, a frown marring his forehead.

"Luke's? Now? Are you sure?"

She nodded determinedly. "Yes, I am."

"But what will you..." His voice trailed off, and to her surprise he paled visibly. "Oh."

She put a hand on his arm, ignoring the tingling sensation under her fingers. *Save it for later*, she thought. *Save it for Luke.*

"I need this, Andrew. Please humor me."

"Gillian…I can't." He took a step back, forcing her to unwillingly remove her hand from his arm. "Please…"

"Why not? Andy, you said it yourself earlier, we are all grownups here. What can you possibly have against me spending an evening with Luke? He's single, and so am I. I doubt even the guard, Mrs. Cooper, would mind."

He didn't respond to her little joke, instead he looked almost nauseous as he backed toward the door.

"Andy…"

His odd, harsh laughter interrupted her. "It has always been Luke, hasn't it? To you it doesn't matter it's been thirteen years. He's still the one you want. The only one you want."

She held out her hands toward him, his strange reaction to her request disturbing her, but he shook his head slowly, with all the world's sadness in his blue eyes.

"No," he whispered. "I can't."

She stared at the empty doorway as he left the house, and a minute later she heard the engine of his truck start after a few coughs, and he drove away with a flying start. Numbly she went up to her room, where she sat down on the bed, trying to sort the mess in her head.

What was Andrew's problem?

He had acted as if the thought of her spending an evening with another man, and maybe passing a couple of bases, hurt him more than she'd thought possible. He was a married man. Why was he acting like this?

She remembered what Luke had said about

Andrew's feelings for her back when they were in high school, but even those shouldn't have made him act like he just had.

As if she was being unfaithful to him.

The problem for her was that, to her surprise, she also felt as if she was being unfaithful to him. Andrew meant more to her than she had known, considering he had been a teenage boy when she had last seen him, and her heart cried over the fact he wasn't for her.

In some weird way Luke was just a substitute for Andrew, but she couldn't tell him that. Not now when he had reacted so strangely to her plans. She hesitated slightly as she reached for her purse. Was this what she wanted? Was she on the right track now, thinking about seducing Luke, if only mentally for now?

Yes.

She wasn't going to get in bed with him because of her mother's hurtful cut, which would be a bad reason to do anything. But she was honest enough about her own feelings and knew she was almost embarrassingly desperate in her childish need to feel wanted.

She clenched her jaw. She was going to do this, because she needed to get it out of her system. Luke was a perfect pawn to use for the occasion. He was the love of her childhood, and maybe this was what she needed—to be able to get over the past and finally start to see a future for herself.

Daisy's room was empty, just as she had assumed it would be, and she grabbed her cell phone to call the neighbors. They confirmed her daughter was over there, but as she had fallen asleep in front of the TV they wondered if it was possible for her to spend the night at their house.

It was as if the gods were on her side.

After checking in on her sleeping mother and the nurse who sat with her, Gillian dashed out the door and walked briskly back toward the church. She didn't stop until she stood outside the small door, hidden among the rosebushes, which led into the part of the boarding house where the appointed clergyman lived.

Staring at the door, she hesitated for a moment with her hand in the air, ready to knock. Was she sure about this? Was she even ready for this?

She sighed deeply, eyes closed, mustering the willpower she had left. She needed this, if not for herself, at least for Daisy. The girl shouldn't have to grow up without a father or a sibling. And if this was Gillian's chance to not only get Daisy a father but perhaps even her biological father, then what was she waiting for?

With one last deep breath, she let her knuckles hit the dark wood of the door. The door leading to her future.

Chapter Six

Luke's face lit up when he saw who had knocked on his door. "Gillian, come in. I was just pouring myself a glass of wine. Would you like one too?"

"Why not." She closed the door behind her and followed him through the boarding house corridor into his room, where she sank down on the inviting sofa, trying to make herself feel a bit more comfortable.

Handing her a glass filled with red wine, Luke sat down beside her. His brown eyes glistened intensely at her, and she forced a self-assured smile, so he wouldn't see how nervous she was.

"Where's Andy?"

Why did he have to talk about Andrew? Gillian sighed quietly. It was partly to forget about him she had sought Luke out, after all. Having him remind her of the reason for her desperation had not been a part of her game plan.

"Working. He had patients waiting for him."

"But you won't wait for him?"

She shook her head. "No."

"I'm glad to hear that."

"So, I heard you and Mrs. Cooper are an item."

He chuckled, his amused eyes darkening slightly in the dim light. "You could say we are. Luckily for me, she's still living in her own small house down on the other side of town, even though she's constantly trying to persuade me to let her stay in one of the guest rooms for good. Thank God I haven't fallen into that trap yet. If I had, I wouldn't have been able to ask you to come in. Mrs. Cooper would have destroyed any chance of me having a normal life."

"A watchdog, or whatever it was Matthew called her?"

"Yes. And very insightful, for Matthew. She *is* a watchdog, but a welcome one. If you only knew how much unwilling attention I get from the ladies nowadays, since I became the head of the church here in Barnesville. Even some of the married ladies lay nets for me, trying to drag me into their plush arms, hoping I will save them from the tediousness of everyday life. Mrs. Cooper makes the balance between spiritual leader and unwilling Casanova work out."

He looked down into his glass, swirling the wine absentmindedly, and she bit her lip as she noticed a familiar air about him. Although he looked perfectly at ease, leaned back in the sofa with his long legs crossed at the ankles in front of him, she still could sense a wry awareness inside him. It was as if he couldn't relax completely due to some deep need to be on his guard.

Something was definitely bothering him, something he had hidden so well from everyone else that it was slowly eating him up from inside. She knew what it was like, to never be able to let go. She had lived like that most of her life, yearning for some kind of approval from Rachel.

She had never received any, and here she was, thirty-one years old and still waiting in the shadows, watching her mother's every move in search of any little sign telling her she did matter.

"I'm glad you have removed the collar," she teased him in an attempt to make him lose his odd somberness. "I'm still in shock over you becoming a clergyman, and that would have been a little too much, I think."

His crooked smile warmed her as he lost his wistfulness. "I don't use it at home. My faith and my deep belief in the Lord are in my heart. It most definitely doesn't come from something I wear under my chin. But the patronesses of the church did insist, and who am I to let a lady in distress down. Or, in this case, a whole bunch of them."

"I feel for you. It can't be easy to deal with the likes of Sally Barnes and my mother every day. They are so used to having it their way, the traditional way. It must be hard for you to come up with something new, to change anything."

"Are you swearing in the rectory?" His eyes sparkled toward her. "Did you, Gillian Crane, use that awful word that should be erased from every dictionary and the English language—*change*?"

"That bad, huh?"

"They are impossible. But I work slowly. I have infiltrated their minds with small ideas hidden deep beneath their thoughts about how it should be, and I'm sensing a possible route to something new. And after all, they can't live forever, now, can they? Sooner or later they will die and I can do whatever I wish. Oh, sorry…"

He grimaced uncomfortably as he caught what he had just said. But she bit back sadness and pretended to not notice the bad joke. "I don't think Sally Barnes ever will die. She's a demon from hell, and she will rule this town with her bony fingers until the end of time."

"You don't like her?"

She shook her head. "No, never have. She's my mother's cousin and close friend, and I spent a lot of time with her during my childhood. Then I just found her awful, always interfering, and nagging about my clothes, my hair, or anything she could think of. But now... As an adult it strikes me how cold she is and how calculatingly she acts. Every move she makes, every word she says has been specifically chosen. She's never spontaneous or affectionate. Not even toward her only child."

"Maybe he has inherited her dark side?"

She smiled reluctantly over his choice of words. "No, I don't think so. Matthew has been known to show kindness now and then, even though you can count the times on one hand's fingers. He's an overbearing bully for sure, but that's just because he doesn't know any better."

"You know, to an outsider your mother seems just as cold and untouchable." His grin warmed the subject, and she shrugged lightly.

"I know. And in some ways she is. But the difference between the two of them is that where Sally never does anything for anyone else, my mother does. She's the one who has fought hard all her adult life about collecting money and goods for different charities, and that's something Sally finds absolutely unnecessary."

"You're right." He frowned as he thought about what she said, looking more handsome than ever. "As you so well put it, your mother *does* think about others, almost obsessively so, whereas Sally never does anything for anyone else if she isn't more or less forced to, or unless it makes her look the better person."

"Nothing can make that woman look better."

Again he flashed his crooked grin, and her teenage heart fluttered in response. Slowly he moved closer to her, his eyes sizzling her with their heat.

"But you sure do."

She swallowed hard with anticipation. "That's the wine talking."

"Well, pour me some more wine then." His husky laughter echoed inside her, and she was almost purring with satisfaction over his attentiveness.

Grabbing her by the waist, he pulled her closer to him. Slowly she lifted her arms and put them around his neck, letting her hands run through his thick hair as she had dreamt so much about doing all those years ago.

"Are you sure about this?" he asked, sounding just as hesitant as she felt, and she nodded, repressing the nagging reluctance at the back of her mind.

At first neither of them noticed the phone ringing, as his lips slowly moved closer to hers, but in the end they couldn't ignore the loud noise, and with a sigh Luke leaned back from her, lifting the receiver to his ear.

"Walker."

Sitting back, feeling oddly relieved, she watched the warmth vanish from Luke's face as dry somberness took over. Something had happened, and with a lump in her throat she waited silently, fearing it was news about her mother. Her eyes questioned him as he hung up the phone.

"There's been an accident over at the old mill, a truck crashing into a bus. There are people asking for a priest, and so…"

His voice trailed off, his eyes already darting around the room, searching for the things he needed with him.

"Can I help?"

"That would be great." His obvious gratefulness over her easy acceptance of the end of their moment nearly escaped her notice. "Grab a jacket for yourself over there at the rack, and go out into the kitchen and put the kettle on. The water will boil faster in it than in the pan."

She rushed to do as asked, and soon she sat in his car with a basket filled with towels, blankets, and two thermoses filled with hot water. Driving as fast as the narrow, winding roads allowed, through the dark Connecticut countryside, neither of them spoke a word until they saw the blinking lights from the many emergency vehicles that had accumulated.

"My God," Luke whispered as he saw the bodies lying covered with blankets, telling them death had already taken their poor souls. "I-I have to go see where I can be of assistance."

He left her standing in the midst of the dead bodies, and she felt tears prick her eyes. All these persons had died too early, leaving families behind that now would have to learn to live without them.

"Are you hurt?"

A woman, obviously a nurse, grabbed hold of Gillian's chin and forced her to meet her eyes.

"N-no," she stuttered, meeting the competent stare. "Can I help in some way? I have hot water and blankets…"

"Honey, you are a godsend. If you go down there to the ambulance, you will find a large man with blond hair. That's Doctor Marshall. He will need what you have."

Gillian stared numbly across the road toward the blinking ambulance. "Andy's here?"

The nurse didn't answer, just waved her hand in the right direction and continued her search for people in need. Gillian swallowed deeply before making her way through the chaotic scene, searching for Andrew.

"Gilly." Andrew's tired eyes lit up as he saw her. "You are a sight for sore eyes. What are you doing here?"

"They needed Luke."

"Ah. Yes, there have been a lot of casualties. Why aren't there more seatbelts in busses? Look at all these wounded people. You'd think it was a war zone, not a quiet countryside road. It's such a waste."

He dried his forehead with the back of his hand, and she winced as she noticed the blood on his gloves.

"Not mine," Andrew said when he noticed her distress. Quickly he removed the gloves and threw them into a trash bin behind him. "I was called here just as your Luke was."

She didn't like the way he said *your* Luke. It sounded almost like an insult. But she didn't stress the matter. This was not the time or the place to pinpoint words or how they were pronounced. Being a doctor on the scene of an accident like this had to be awful and straining, and so she put a hand on his arm comfortingly.

"Can I help you in any way?"

He ran his fingers through his hair, tousling the blond tresses even more. "Can you go with me? The nurses are too busy with doing a first and second check on the injured, and I need someone to fetch me things."

His warm smile washed over her as she nodded, and he pointed toward a bag by his car. "There's an extra robe in that bag. Put it on, and then come back to join me."

It was a night she would never forget.

Slowly she and Andrew moved from one person to another, taking care of bloody gashes and straightening broken limbs. Silently they worked together, as if Gillian had a sixth sense when it came to his needs, and she was there with items ready for him when he needed them.

The patients loved him, and she couldn't blame them. Who wouldn't love a doctor who looked like an overgrown angel? Gillian was sure his large hands and warm smile helped just as much as the medical care he gave.

She looked at Luke sitting with the victims in need of spiritual guidance, holding their hands while reading to them from the Bible. It was a strange picture, although she had to admit that he somehow did fit into his new role perfectly.

Some people never ceased to surprise her.

"He does a great job," Andrew said, following her gaze as he caught her staring at their friend.

"Yes, he does."

"You look surprised."

She grimaced, embarrassed. "I guess I still have a hard time seeing the Luke I used to know as a man of the cloth. I keep forgetting none of us are the same as we were thirteen years ago."

"We all have changed, for better or worse. I can only hope you don't find us all less than what you used to think."

Beyond tired, he was still trying to cheer her up with a joke, it seemed, and to please him she forced a smile. "Can't say so much about the others yet, but you, Andrew Marshall, are even more lovable than you were when I left."

Instead of teasing her back, he looked at her seriously. "I'm sorry your date with Luke was interrupted. I know how much he means to you."

She shrugged absentmindedly, following Luke with her eyes as he moved to the next crying victim. "This is more important than trying to find out if we were meant to be. We can do that whenever."

"Interrupted too soon, then?"

She looked back at him, frowning over his almost too satisfied tone of voice. "Too soon for what?"

This time it was he who shrugged, almost daintily, as if he didn't care at all what her answer would be. "I imagine you hadn't much time to do some real finding out."

Gillian could hardly believe her ears. "Are you standing here asking me if I had time to have sex with Luke?"

"No, of course not." His laughter was forced and stiff, not fooling her for a minute.

"Yes, you were!" Angrier than she'd been for a long time, she put her hands on her hips as she looked at him with contempt. "You just asked me if I had sex with Luke."

"Gillian—"

"Don't even try." She cut off his response as she turned her back to him, not able to stand by his side any longer. She didn't get far, though. After two steps he grabbed her arm, forcing her to stop and look at him.

"Don't you care at all that you are hurting me so badly with all this? You and Luke together..." He took a deep, staggering breath. "It's like my worst nightmare come true. And you just walk all over me like I mean nothing to you. Hell, you even asked me to take you to your little date!"

She had never seen him this angry. Not toward her, at least. Unfortunately, his anger only increased hers, and she ripped her arm loose from his hand, waving her index finger toward him. "You should be ashamed of yourself, Doctor Marshall. I haven't done anything wrong, whilst you go against every unsaid rule when it comes to love and marriage. What can possibly be wrong with me wanting to see if Luke can make me feel the way I do when I'm with you? You know as well as I do that I can never have you—you are a married man!"

Dazed, he took a step closer to her, his voice only a hoarse whisper. "The way you feel with...*me*?"

She crossed her arms as if trying to build a shield against him. All her anger flew away, and suddenly she felt too tired to think. Too much had happened during the last day, and all she wanted to do was go home and bury herself in her bed. Alone with her erratic thoughts and aching heart.

"Please leave me alone."

He ignored her quiet plea and put his hands against her cheeks, looking down at her with a strange mix of pain and hope. "Tell me I didn't mishear you telling me I mean more to you than Luke. That my touch makes you feel more than his does."

"Andy..."

69

"Tell me."

"Doctor Marshall, you are needed over at the ambulance."

A nurse's clipped voice shattered the intensity between them, and Gillian grabbed the opportunity, moving backwards and thus effectively removing Andrew's trembling hands from her burning cheeks.

He started to follow her, all caught up in the hurricane of feelings between them, but the nurse didn't dawdle. Grimly she walked up and put herself in front of Andrew. "*Now*, Doctor Marshall. It's an *emergency*."

Hesitantly he started in the direction of the ambulance, still unable to tear his eyes from Gillian. Not until the nurse more or less pushed him toward the ambulance did he throw himself into the action. Relieved, Gillian watched him disappear, then staggered the opposite way, trying to get as far away from him as possible.

What had she done?

Why had she spilled the truth to him? This definitely didn't make her life any easier. Having Andrew nursing old feelings for her in secrecy was one thing, but having Andrew openly and boldly craving her was another. His immediate reaction when she had blurted out what was in her heart had told her all about how the future would be. He would never be able to let this go, not without talking it through thoroughly with her, demanding that she let him have a chance to rethink his choice of life.

She didn't want that.

She was too tired to talk, too tired to think. She just needed her bed, preferably with a chatty Daisy in it, telling her about all the exciting things she'd been through and so pushing all matters of the heart aside again.

Far, far aside.

As she started back toward town, the sky was painted red and orange from the fire still burning in the vehicles involved in the accident. Cars stood still alongside the road, frightened people staring at the accident site, not able to hide the fascination that had drawn them there.

"Gillian!"

Megan Barnes waved from one of the cars in the back, beckoning Gillian to join her, and she obliged tiredly, unable to resist the chance of maybe catching a ride back to town.

"Hi, Megan."

"My God, Gillian, you look absolutely freezing. Here, take off that dirty smock and put on Matt's jacket instead. I forgot to take it inside when I brought it home from the drycleaners today. Matt keeps telling me I'm such a forgetful whimsy, but now I'm glad I am. Put it on and get into the car. You look like you're about to faint."

She had forgotten she wore Andrew's robe. Looking down at the now dirty white doctor's smock as she removed it, Gillian resisted an urge to lift it to her nose and inhale the scent of him. Instead she put on Matthew's warm jacket with trembling hands before getting into the car with Megan.

"Do you need a ride home?" Megan asked, her Samaritan heart reaching out to her friend.

"That would be great, Megan. Thank you."

"I was on my way home anyway. Matt had me drive him here so that as mayor he could help take care of the victims and talk with the press when they show up."

Of course Matthew Barnes wanted to be here. Accidents as horrible as this one were like magnets to the media. Without a doubt they would come barging into the usually very uninteresting town of Barnesville after this news, and for someone as hungry for attention as Matthew it meant interviews and perhaps a photo of himself in a national newspaper.

Gillian couldn't help wondering what he was like as a husband and a father. Parenthood meant prioritizing someone else before yourself—something she could imagine Matthew might have a problem with. She glanced into the empty back seat. "Where are the girls?"

"They are with Candy. I'm so grateful for having her. She's the best aunt there is, not to mention sister. She's saved me more times than I can count."

Megan's fragile beauty lit up with her radiant smile filled with love, and Gillian couldn't help but smile back. Megan was irresistible when not aloof, and it was so sad she let her husband walk all over her, effectively belittling her into a shadow of the exceptional young woman she had once been.

"I'm pretty sure Candy thinks she has the best sister too," Gillian said with warmth, glad to think about something other than the unnerving clash with Andrew.

Megan blushed, not comfortable with receiving compliments, something Gillian had no problem with relating to; she too felt awkward when someone praised her or her achievements.

"What an awful accident." Megan changed the

subject to the horrors of reality as they left the blinking lights behind them. "All those dead and wounded. My heart goes out to their poor families."

"Mine too. You should have seen the other wreckage behind the burning truck. It was hard to see it even had been a bus. Now it's just a big lump of metal. I might be the most selfish person alive, but I thanked God I knew Daisy hadn't been a part of it, that I know she is safe and alive far from here."

"I did too. When I heard there were several children among the deceased, I went up to the children's bedrooms and watched them breathe calmly in their sleep. I just had to see with my own eyes they were alive and well."

"Must be a special motherly thing." Gillian grinned before yawning loudly.

"Must be. Matt rolled his eyes over my gratitude, but I don't care if he thinks I'm a dimwit—my girls are safe and alive. That's all that matters."

Gillian yawned again, a long, jaws-wide-open yawn, which garnered her an amused look from her driver.

"Feeling a bit drowsy?"

The compassion in Megan's voice made Gillian feel even more exhausted. It had been a long day, and much had happened. Mostly she was tired of thinking and feeling. She longed to sleep and let her brain rest without the constant thoughts about her dying mother, Daisy's unknown father, and her own turbulent feelings when it came to Andrew and Luke.

"I'm so sorry. It's just been too much lately. What happened today brought forward that famous last straw. I thought I was stronger than this, but…"

Her voice trailed off, as no words could describe what a failure she felt.

"Why don't you come home with me, stay over at our house tonight? We can drive by your mother's house on the way and pick Daisy up. She can stay in the fourth bed in the girls' room—they would be absolutely ecstatic to find her there in the morning. You can sleep in our guest room and soak in the tub until you look like a raisin. Tomorrow the girls and I will spoil you with freshly made scones for breakfast, and we can talk. I...I think we both need that."

It was such a thoughtful offer, coming from a caring heart. Gillian felt tears prick her eyes as she, to her surprise, found it absolutely alluring. To be able to leave the sordid atmosphere of her mother's house and for one night stay somewhere else. A house in which laughter was allowed and where the rooms were made to use, not just for display.

A home.

"Are you sure?" she asked carefully, not wanting to become too thrilled about the idea until she knew it was honestly meant, although Megan wasn't known for being a liar, rather for being too honest for her own good.

"Of course I am. It would be so much fun. A reminder of the old days, you know, when you, me, and Candy would have a sleepover in our room."

"I'm not so fun now, I'm afraid."

Megan laughed, the radiance of her beauty reappearing. "No one will be expecting anything of you tonight. I assure you I will keep myself as far away from you as possible. But tomorrow, that's a whole different story. So will you come?"

"I can't deny such an appealing offer. But I must disappoint your daughters, as Daisy is on a sleepover already at a friend's house."

"Then what they don't know…"

After calling her mother's nurse to inform her of her whereabouts, Gillian closed her eyes and didn't open them again until Megan turned off the engine outside the Barnes's house. As if she could feel Gillian's need of solitude, Megan simply showed her the guest room and its adjoining bathroom before leaving Gillian. On her way out the bedroom door, she indicated a pile of clean clothes Gillian was welcome to wear the next day.

"Lock the door. As soon as the girls hear about you being here, they will come, and I promise you, you don't want them in bed with you in the morning. If I say bouncing balls, I think you get the picture."

Exhausted, Gillian said goodnight to her friend and locked the door tightly, though the thought of three happy little girls sounded considerably better to her than Megan probably thought.

That night she slept like a baby for the first time since she had come to Barnesville. The bath had been wonderful, relaxing her so much she fell asleep in the tub. She didn't wake up until the water started to get cold, her body wrinkly as the raisin Megan had joked about.

As she got dressed, she knew she would never be able to thank Megan enough for this night, for offering her an oasis in the barren desert that was her life. It became clearer by the minute that this trip to her childhood hometown had stirred up more than she had bargained for.

Just having to deal with her mother's upcoming demise and the perpetual lack of warmth between them was enough to stagger anyone. But for Gillian that wasn't enough. No, she had Daisy, too, and her relentless hunt for her father. That girl had more guts than Gillian thought possible and had been everywhere, secretly taking photos of possible men.

She could only hope her daughter would be satisfied with searching from the shadows, secretly investigating possible men. If Daisy decided to take a more radical approach and maybe do something more forward, like showing Gillian's photo, then the whole thing could get really nasty.

And then there was Andrew.

Ever since the day she and Daisy first arrived in Barnesville and met him outside the doctor's office, Gillian had been fascinated with the man her best friend had become. There was just something about him that made her feel at ease, as if she finally had come home.

If he weren't married she knew she would have stalked him until he gave in and became hers forever and ever. But he *was* already spoken for, and to her that meant never-to-be, even though just thinking about letting him go hurt more than she thought possible, considering she had been back in Barnesville for only a little over a week.

And just as she had persuaded herself to flirt with Luke instead, she had managed to blurt out her feelings for Andrew. There was no way he would leave her alone now. It was easy to see he felt more for her than he should, considering he had a wife he was supposed to love and cherish until eternity.

She would have to avoid him as much as possible

for as long as she and Daisy remained in Barnesville, and make sure they never, ever would be alone again. For the first time since her arrival she felt thankful for the Barnesville Hyenas spending as much time as they could in her mother's house, trying to ease her way into death. They were overbearing, patronizing, and plain rude, but now Gillian didn't mind. She wouldn't mind being insulted all day if it meant Andrew couldn't speak with her in private.

Last, but definitely not least, was Luke. Gorgeous, handsome Luke who she had dreamt so much about during her childhood years and now was hers if she wanted.

But something inside of her wasn't as partial to him anymore. It wasn't Luke who made her heart flutter. Someone else had come out from the shadows of her heart and turned upside down all her thoughts about what she really felt.

With a sigh she straightened the bed before collecting her dirty clothes. No use to dwell on this now. Downstairs Megan and her three daughters waited for her, and the delightful scent of the freshly made scones she had been promised was making her hungry.

As she walked down the stairs she knew one thing—she had to avoid being alone with Andrew from now on. No matter what he tried or what he said, she would have to stay as far away from him as possible. Luckily she now was in Megan's home, and when she had to go back to her mother's house later on, she hoped there would be enough hyenas there for her to hide behind.

Chapter Seven

"So, Matthew Barnes, eh?"

"No big surprise there." Megan made a small, awkward grimace Gillian supposed was meant to be a smile as she poured a cup of coffee for her guest. "We were made for each other, you know. The popular quarterback and the cheerleading homecoming queen—a perfect match made in high school heaven."

"You make it sound as if you married him because you had to, not because you wanted to."

"Of course I wanted to marry him," Megan said with a slightly irritated tone. "Matthew was the most popular guy in school, every girl wanted him."

"Not all. I never did."

Again Megan smiled her honest, radiant smile. "You weren't supposed to be in love with him; you're his second cousin, after all. And besides, everyone knew you had a thing for Luke."

"And there I was all those years ago, thinking you had a thing for Jake Storm."

A fierce blush crept over Megan's smooth cheeks, confirming the rumor without words. Not that she needed to, though. It had been so obvious back then how she fancied Jake above all the other boys. Not once did she say anything about it, but no one who saw the two of them together could have missed the attraction between them.

The chemistry had been too obvious—electrifying.

The only problem had been that Jake was Matthew's best friend, and as Matthew had already marked Megan as his... It saddened Gillian a bit that the love story hadn't had another outcome, especially as the Matt and Megan didn't seem to be particularly happy together. Who knew what Megan would have been today, if she had ended up with Jake instead of Matthew.

"So," Megan said pointedly, changing the subject away from herself. "Luke Walker, eh?"

"We're not an item, if that's what you mean."

Megan grinned, lifting her cup of coffee. "I didn't think you would be an item yet. As far as I know, you just met him again, didn't you?"

Gillian bit off a big chunk of still-warm scone, trying to stall the interrogation a bit. "Uh-huh."

"But you did go with him from the diner."

"Uh-huh."

"And I heard you spent quite some time in the church alone with him."

Were they already gossiping about her, keeping track of her whereabouts? Gillian frowned unwillingly. It was a scary thought that it didn't have to be more than an innocent meeting in a church to unleash the wagging tongues of Barnesville.

Megan must have noticed Gillian's discomfort, and she quickly continued, "Sally collects every tidbit she hears swirling in the grapevine, and as she still hasn't given up on the ridiculous thought that I one day will be just as crude and interfering as she is, she tends to tell me every last one of them."

"You have my deepest sympathy."

"For what?" Megan's laughter echoed in the cozy kitchen, and her daughters looked up from their coloring books to smile with their mother.

Gillian lowered her voice so the girls sitting at the kitchen table wouldn't hear. "For living with Sally around the corner."

"Ah, yes." Megan sighed, and beckoned Gillian to follow her further away from the children so they could talk freely without small ears overhearing every word. "If there ever was anyone deserving a medal for Unbelievable Services to Human Kind it would be me. She's dreadful."

"I'm so sorry, Megan. Knowing what she's like, I can just imagine how difficult it must be, having to be nice to her, to let her into your home and listen to her dissecting how you do things."

"Oh, she doesn't say much about how I *am* doing things. She's much more partial to telling me how I *should* do things. Especially when it comes to the children. Sally thinks I am ruining them completely by being too soft, and that's why they are such, and I quote, snappy small monsters who just can't shut up."

"Sounds like she's just like my mother and thinks highly of the old saying that children shall be seen and not heard."

"Oh, yes. She has told me countless times how I should not ask them so much about their day. She figures that by doing so I make them think their thoughts actually are worth listening to and therefore they will strain everyone's ears with their nonsense."

Speechless, Gillian stared at Megan, not understanding how she could stand such narrow-mindedness from anyone, and from her mother-in-law of all people.

"Has she ever told the girls…?"

"Good Lord, no. If she had, I would have forbidden her to ever see them again. I think she knows that and therefore insists on pinpointing me about it instead."

To Gillian such behavior was intolerable. She would have made the cut with Sally a long time ago. But then again, she had no mother-in-law, so she hadn't a clue how it was to have one around.

"What about Matthew? How does he handle this?"

"He's not handling it at all. You could say he's like an ostrich, hiding his head in the sand and pretending it doesn't happen. It drives me crazy, but then again—Sally is behaving just as awful toward him, too, so I can't blame him for it. I've never heard her praise him once during all these years. She just constantly nags about his wrongdoings and shortcomings."

"Poor Matthew! But then, I'm not surprised. She is the devil in disguise. I must say, I admire you two. You've managed to make your relationship work despite her."

"Who says it's working?"

It was just a mumble, not meant to be heard, but Gillian caught it anyway. So there was sand in the machinery, just as she had thought. Her heart went out to Megan, who must feel as if caught between plague and cholera.

"How bad is it?"

Megan shrugged, tears in her eyes. "I honestly don't know. Matt refuses to talk to me about our relationship so he can continue pretending everything's fine. It feels like I live in some sort of no-man's land with a husband who says or does anything which can save him from actually facing what a cold joke our marriage has become."

There were no words to say. All Gillian could do was offer her compassion, and so she put her arms around Megan's shaking body and hugged her close. Quietly, so she wouldn't alert the girls, Megan cried out all her angst, and all Gillian could do was stroke her back and murmur something inaudible meant to soothe.

"Love hurts so much," Megan whispered between sobs as she finally left Gillian's embrace. "I don't want to love anymore."

"Mommy!" Katie squealed, over at the kitchen table, effectively interrupting the tension. "Mandy took the red pen from my hand. I want it back—it was mine!"

Mandy stuck her tongue out toward her sister, unaware she was being watched, and in seconds Megan stood by her daughter's side, waving her index finger— the utter picture of maternity.

The rest of the morning they played with the two older girls and cuddled with baby Ellie, not mentioning the emotional moment. But Gillian could feel her relationship to Megan had changed. They now had a deep, invisible bond between them, and it made Gillian sad to think she would lose this newfound friendship when she went back home to New York again.

"Promise me you'll come by again," Megan said as she hugged Gillian goodbye after they'd had a fun, although a somewhat stain-filled, lunch in the girls' playhouse.

"I will. Katie promised me she would let me hold her dolly, and who am I to decline such a generous offer?"

Leaving the Barnes residence, Gillian felt more relaxed than she had in weeks. Luckily for her, Matthew had had too much to do with the accident and hadn't come home for the night. That man was an ogre.

She looked at the church tower rising high above the roofs of the houses of Barnesville. Would Luke or Andrew handle a strained marriage so coldly? She didn't think so. But then again, she would never have thought Matthew would have, either. And yet he did.

"What a sad little face," Candice said as Gillian came into the diner and sat down on a high stool at the counter. "Is your mother worse?"

Accepting a cup of hot coffee, Gillian shook her head. "No, according to the nurse, my mother is still the same today, slowly dying but still alive."

"Yikes." Candice grimaced. "You make me glad I was too small to remember when my mother died. But on the other hand, you have memories of yours. I only have photos that don't mean much to me."

A new customer arrived, and with an apology Candice left Gillian to meet him, seeing him to a booth where she poured him a cup of coffee while taking his order. Gillian watched her old friend as she moved around the diner, joking and waitressing, making sure everyone had what they needed.

It didn't matter how much Matthew made fun of her, Candice was excellent as a waitress. She might have a hard time telling men to stay out of her bed, but that was a completely different thing and had nothing to do with her job.

"Everyone is so rattled over the horrible accident yesterday. Good Lord, I'm so glad no one I know and love was caught in it." Candice sat down beside Gillian, grabbing a fresh salad from the counter, grinning when she noticed her friend's curious look. "Time for lunch. Want anything?"

"No, thank you. I just had lunch over at your sister's. She and the girls spoiled me rotten, served their best cheese and macaroni."

Candice lit up. "My lovely little girls. They are my reason for living. Conniving little monsters, for sure, but I do love them until eternity. So did you get a good night's rest?"

"Yes, as a matter of fact, I did. Slept like a baby. I didn't know I was so tense until Megan gave me somewhere to breathe."

"Megan's good at that. She should work as a nurse or something else that means taking care of people."

"Must run in the family. You are exceptionally good with what you do, Candy. You make every last customer smile."

"That's me, you know, doing everything I can to satisfy. According to Matthew, I do even more to make the men feel welcomed and pleased."

"Don't take what Matthew says to heart. He's just a bully who says anything he can think of to hurt you."

"I know." Candice sighed, her usually cheerful face dark and wounded. "But unfortunately I can't overlook it, because he speaks the truth. I have been more than welcoming to too many masculine guests in the past, and now I just can't get that undone. I will have to live the rest of my life knowing every last citizen of Barnesville thinks less of me for it. I've been called the town slut to my face by Sally and her bitches, and no matter what I say, everyone agrees with them."

"I don't." Gillian put a supporting hand on top of

Candice's.

"Of course you don't. You haven't been here the last decade to see my fall from grace with your own eyes. The sad thing is that my too lecherous lifestyle in my early twenties now has me a pariah among any men here in Barnesville and the surrounding communities who might be searching for a wife. All I want is to find a man who wants to spend the rest of his life in my arms and won't think one night is enough."

"Go somewhere else, then, to find a man. Use the dating services online. I have lots of friends back in New York who have found their partners through those."

"Don't you think I've tried?" Candice laughed hollowly. "Everything's just fine until I bring them here, introduce them to my home and the people who live here. Not one has lasted a day after meeting the philistine minds of Barnesville."

It was so sad. The beautiful, warmhearted Candice deserved to be loved and to be able to love back. Somewhere there had to be a man who could overlook her past and cherish her for the wonderful person she was.

"There must be someone…"

"Old Grandpa Brown told me the other day he would marry me if no one else ever understood what a gem I am when it comes to making good coffee."

"You could do worse."

Candice's laughter filled the diner, and eyes turned their way, curiously taking in who had the waitress laughing so hard.

The door opened, and Gillian's heart skipped a beat as she caught something blond in the corner of her eye.

Relief mixed with frustration as she saw it was a stranger and not Andrew.

Why was she unconsciously looking for him? The sole reason for her sitting here was to avoid going home and happening to bump into him. She wasn't ready to face him and have to explain her confession yesterday.

"What's bothering you, Gillian?"

She met Candice's concerned eyes, and the need to share what was in her heart overwhelmed her. She knew Candice, and she wasn't the gossiping type, especially because of how she was treated by those who were.

Before she could stop herself, Gillian took a deep breath and blurted out the one word expressing all her angst. "Andy."

Candice's eyebrows arched with surprise over the answer. "*Andy?* Why is he bothering you? Has it to do with your mother?"

"No. Just with Andy."

"Oh." Candice looked stunned. "You two… Are you…?"

"No! And we never will."

"You won't? W-why?"

"Because… You know!"

Candice shook her head. "No. I don't. I really don't get why not. When I think about it, you are like made for each other. Best friends since forever, his mother loves you almost more than she loves him, and he's the sweetest man there is. You couldn't do better."

"Really, Candy?" Gillian gasped. "You actually think it's okay for him to leave everything for me? That others get hurt so I can be happy?"

"Yes, because I don't see the problem. Everybody

knows he loves you. He always has, so the problem can't be with him. It must be you, then. Are you married?"

"What? No!"

"Maybe you just don't care for Andrew."

Gillian was starting to get really annoyed. "Of course I do. There wouldn't be a problem if I didn't, would there now?"

"No. You're right. Well, then I just can't see the problem. Here you are, two adults who apparently love each other. What could possibly be wrong with that?"

"His wife!"

"Wife? You're having a problem with Wife? Why? She'll get used to the whole thing. Just give her some time."

Gillian didn't know what to say. How could Candice sit there coldly dismissing Andrew's wife as if she wasn't worth considering? What had the poor woman ever done against Candice to receive such a treatment? Or maybe it was Candice's liberal-minded attitude toward love that colored her opinion.

"Well, I can't live like that, knowing I'm the sole reason for so much heartache. It would affect my feelings for Andrew, and in the end I fear I would feel too disgusted about the whole thing."

"I think you are making one big mistake here, and it angers me how you so lightly deny yourself what I long for so much—love."

"Candice…"

"So you won't do anything about it, then? Poor Andy! He sure is worth so much more than this."

Gillian felt tears prick her eyes, and she regretted her rash decision to open up her heart to Candice. "I think *I* deserve much more than this. I deserve a man who will stand by me and not someone who too easily will leave one relationship for another. That's not a man I could trust with all my emotional baggage, and that's just the thing—I desperately need someone to trust. I need someone to rely on. I'm sorry, Candy, but I just couldn't live with a man who doesn't respect marriage. I have Daisy to think about. I don't want her to have to say goodbye to him because he finds someone else he fancies more after he's been with me a while."

Angrier than Gillian had ever seen her before, Candice put her cup down hard on the wooden counter. "It's Andrew Marshall we're talking about," she hissed so no one of the openly staring diner guests would hear. "Your Andy, who has loved you since the first day you two met and who would never hurt a fly, and you even less."

"But he would hurt *his wife*!"

Candice was starting to look really confused. "Gillian, honey. Why are you so obsessed with Wife? She shouldn't be…"

"No! Just stop it, Candy," Gillian interrupted, too upset to care about being rude. "It's much better for me to find someone else, someone who always will be there for me. Like Luke, who is free to love and free to make a commitment."

"Luke?" Candice stared openmouthed at her. "Why would you go after Luke when you have Andy?"

"Why not? He's a good man and would make a wonderful husband and father."

"B-but you want Andy, don't you? Why go after L-Luke if your heart's not in it?"

Gillian's eyes narrowed as she stared at Candice.

Something was wrong. Something was definitely wrong. Why was Candice looking like Gillian was stabbing her in the heart over and over and over again? It was almost as if…

"Oh, my God, you are in love with Luke!"

Chapter Eight

The fierce blush creeping over Candice's cheeks told the truth, even though she immediately shook her head in denial. "No, I'm not."

"Yes, you are. You are in love with Lucas Walker."

Candice lowered her voice until she almost hissed again. "I am *not* in love with him."

Gillian leaned forward until her nose almost touched Candice's. "Yes. You. Are."

Candice looked ready to cry but didn't persist in keeping up her fake indifference. Instead she sat back and sighed heavily, closing her eyes as if in despair.

"Come on, Candice. Anyone can see how much you care. Your heart is in your eyes."

"Please, promise me you won't tell anyone."

Gillian softened as she heard Candice's heartfelt wish. "I won't."

"Thank you."

They sat silent for the longest of times. Gillian didn't dare to move, too afraid to scare her friend off. There was a story here, and Gillian was a sucker for love stories.

Just as she was about to give up, Candice opened her mouth, her voice tight and insecure.

"All right. I admit it—I am in love with Luke. Always have been, always will be. But he has never seen me. Not once during all these years we have known each other has he reacted to me in any way other than with absentminded friendship. Not until lately, that is. A few weeks ago, he happened to come in here when I was alone, and at first we just chatted away as we always have, talking about this and that. But suddenly he became quiet and just stared at me with those beautiful brown eyes. It was as if he'd seen me for the first time and really liked what he saw." Candice sighed deeply, her voice shaking as she continued. "H-he never said anything about it, but you know how it is, you *know* when someone wants you. From that day on, he started to come here more often, and every time it felt as if he came closer to asking me out."

"Why didn't you ask him?" Gillian wondered, her head filled with the lovely image of Luke and Candice silently yearning for each other.

"Because I'm Candice Lee, the unpaid whore of Barnesville. I was just too afraid to come on to him. I didn't want to make him think he was just one amongst many. And maybe because I too want to know how it feels to be the wanted maiden, to have a man court *me* until marriage is the only way out. And you know what? It felt as if we were heading there, Luke and me, even though he never said anything about it."

"So what happened?"

Candice's smile was just as crooked as Luke's, only sadder. "You came back."

"Me? I don't understand…"

"Oh, come on, Gillian. When we were kids, all you ever talked about was Luke, and I never could tell you how much I too fancied him, because somehow it felt as if he was all yours. Everyone knew about how you felt, probably Luke too, so how could I tell you I loved him too?" Sighing, Candice rubbed her eyes tiredly. "When you two met yesterday, it was clear as day he was attracted to you, and there was definitely no doubt you returned the attraction in full. His eyes never left your face once, staring dreamily at you just as weeks earlier he had stared at me. As soon as you walked through the door I became invisible to him. It was all about you, just as it had been when we were kids."

Hurting Candice was the last thing Gillian ever wanted to do, but somehow she had done so without even knowing about it. She hadn't been aware of the circumstances, so she shouldn't feel this guilty, but yet she still did.

It became clearer and clearer by the minute how she must have been the most selfish friend there ever was. Gillian sat back, feeling absolutely crushed over how self-centered she had been in high school.

Not only had she completely missed that Andrew had been in love with her—her very best friend she had shared everything with—but now it was quite obvious it had been a one-way sharing. And she was the one to blame, not he. She had been so caught up in her feelings for Luke and her loneliness at home that she never once had asked Andrew how he felt, never asked him if there was a girl he liked, a girl he carried in his heart.

And now Candice…

"I'm so sorry, Candy. I just didn't know."

Snorting softly, Candice blinked away the telling tears in her eyes. "How could you have known? I never said anything, did I?"

"I could have asked."

"We were teenage girls, Gillian. They never think of anyone but themselves. You should know. You're raising one yourself, aren't you?"

"Yeah, she's almost a teen, anyway. But still. It must have been so painful for you, listening to me talking about Luke when he was all you wanted, too."

"Not really." Candice laughed, the sparkle returning to her eyes. "I kind of loved talking about him, you know. And all those times we stalked him… Let's just say I didn't care much about your part of it. To me it was all about him."

The bell above the door rang as another couple entered the diner, interrupting the conversation. Candice excused herself, seeming almost relieved to think about something else. As she walked over to the new guests, welcoming them to the diner, Gillian watched her absentmindedly.

She was so lost in her thoughts she missed the door opening again, and not until someone sat down in the chair Candice had just left did she wake up and look straight into Luke's warm eyes.

"Thinking of me?"

Instinctively her eyes sought out Candice, who stood with her back toward them, taking the couple's orders, unaware of the newcomer.

"Not really, I'm afraid," Gillian said honestly, and he laughed out loud. Candice's back stiffened as she heard the familiar voice, but she didn't turn around, still focused upon her job.

"What was it that had you looking so dreamy, then?" His honest interest was alluring, and she had to stop herself from falling into the same trap again. She had loved him with all her heart when she was young and had already found out how easily she could make herself think she still did.

But the truth was she didn't.

To be completely honest, it still was the same thing as with all her old Barnesville friends: She didn't know the man. She could recognize a good man when she saw him, but it didn't mean she loved him.

Although... Falling in love with him would probably be as easy as falling out of love with him. He was an adorable man, attractive, attentive, and such a heartthrob. But knowing what she knew now, about Candice's feelings for him and them having a good thing going before she arrived, made her decide to stifle those feelings.

Her heart, much to her surprise, already belonged to Andrew. Maybe it was better for her to concentrate on finding out how to fall out of love with *him*, instead of moving all her longing for love to Luke.

"I was thinking about old times and how I'm constantly taking for granted that the people of my acquaintance here stayed the same as they were when I left. Every time I'm talking to someone I become surprised over how different they are now from when I last saw them. That is, everyone except my mother, who is too much as she was when I left. As a matter of fact, if she had the strength I think she would have sent me away all over again."

"Which reminds me." Luke picked up his cell phone. "I promised to text Andy if I met you. He had something he needed to talk to you about."

Oh, God, no.

"Don't," she said hoarsely, stressing her tired brain to find an acceptable excuse. "I'll look him up on the way home. I'm too tired to wait around here for him. If it's all right with you?"

"Of course." Luke's crooked smile warmed her as he put the cell phone back into his pocket. "Do you need a ride? I didn't notice your car outside."

"Why not." Gillian glanced at Candice, but her friend still hadn't turned around, keeping her stiff back toward them as if just seeing the two of them together hurt too much. "I'll just tell Candice I'm leaving. I'll be right with you."

As Luke left the diner, Gillian went up to Candice, waiting impatiently for her to finish her flirting with the guests. When she finally did, she marched up to the counter and put down her notepad hard on the shiny wood.

"Having fun, I hear."

"Candice…"

"Don't say it. I'm not in the mood for your weak excuses. Just go. Go and have a wonderful time with the man of our hearts."

"He offered to drive me home. That's all. I'm not in love with him, and he is not in love with me. We are just friends."

Candice snorted as she ripped a piece of paper off the notepad and gave it to the chef. "Friends with benefits, then."

"He's my friend, Candice, just as you are. I am not going to seduce him just because I used to love him when I was a child. Don't you remember what I told you? It's not him I'm having feelings for."

The steam went out of Candice, and her shoulders slumped as she sent Gillian an embarrassed look. "I'm so sorry. I don't know what I was thinking. I know I'm a bit cautious when it comes to you and Luke, and I guess I have to learn to not be so anymore. Things have changed since our school days, but it's just that my heart can't deal with the fact that you are—or were—a competitor."

"Well, this competitor is going to catch a ride back home and, when there, try to avoid a certain doctor who seems to be hovering about, waiting for me."

"Awkward."

"Tell me about it. I don't know how I'm going to survive this, having him there every day."

"I can't believe I'm about to say what I am going to say, but just as much as you need to get away, I need to do something good for you to ease my embarrassment a bit."

"Okay." Gillian grinned, amused over Candice's wonderful self-irony.

"Why don't you ask Luke if you can stay at the rectory? Not in his bed, mind you, but in the boarding house, where they take in persons in desperate need of a roof over their heads. Mrs. Cooper was here earlier and told me they have a few rooms left even though the accident filled several, so maybe she would have room for you and Daisy."

What a wonderful idea. Gillian felt tears fill her eyes, and she hugged Candice tightly. "Thank you. That would be just what Daisy and I need, to get out of my mother's house. I hate it there, and Daisy does too. It's just too uncomfortable and, sadly enough, we're not wanted there, either. Mother would rest much easier if she knew I was gone."

"You're welcome. But don't forget, though…"

Gillian couldn't hold back a laugh. "I promise you

I will not get in bed with Luke. All right?"

"I suppose so. Now go and get the ball rolling. I'll be over with a bottle of wine later so we can continue our chat. I know I need that."

"Me too, Candy. Me too."

"Great. I'm looking forward to talking with you later, then!"

Gillian was still laughing when she got into Luke's car, and he looked curiously at her. "May I ask what has the lovely Miss Crane giggling like this?"

"Candice. She's such a treat."

"She sure is." He didn't show any emotion, looking as blank as a piece of white paper, something which told her more than anything that his heart was involved.

"Amongst other things, she mentioned you had a couple of extra guest rooms at the rectory's boarding house. Could it be possible you have one available for a single mother and her obnoxious twelve-year-old daughter, for two weeks, at most?"

"Of course I do, but are you sure? It's your mother and your childhood home you would be leaving. Wouldn't you want to stay put there?"

"I hate that house," Gillian mumbled, knowing she had to tell him the truth. "I really, really hate it. It's awful. It's too grand, and more of a museum than a home. And I know my mother doesn't want me there. I think we all would be much happier if I left. I must think of Daisy, too, and I know she will have a much better time here in Barnesville if we leave mother's house."

"Your mother loves you, and I'm sure she wants you to be there, at her side, now as her time is running out."

Gillian shook her head solemnly. "No, she doesn't. And Luke, you don't have to defend her or…or try to find the right words to make me believe she does. I know she cares for me, as much as a person might care for a piece of furniture. I've had ample time during these last thirteen years to come to terms with the fact that she doesn't love me in the normal way a mother loves her child. I can live with that, and I can live with her awful friends, who insist they have all the right in the world to occupy the house any time they wish. But I need to get away from there for Daisy's sake. She deserves more than having to walk around wearing cotton slippers and keeping her voice down and her walk slow."

"That bad, eh?"

"Yes. That bad. So please, Luke. Could we move to rooms at the rectory? It's close enough for me to be at my mother's in a few minutes if needed, but far enough away for us to not feel we are constantly being watched."

"You are so welcome, both you and Daisy. Let's drive back to your mother's house and get your things, and then we can go to the rectory and make you comfortable there, instead."

To Gillian's relief, Andrew was nowhere to be seen when she arrived at the old house. Her mother was asleep, and as her friends hadn't arrived yet, Gillian told the nurse about her new whereabouts and that she would come to sit with her mother the next afternoon.

After picking up an exhilarated Daisy from her friend's house, they went in the direction of the church, to their new home for at least a week or two.

"Are there many bedrooms?" Daisy asked Luke

from the back seat, and he nodded seriously.

"Yes, Miss Daisy, there are plenty of rooms for you to chose from in the boarding house. All the different sizes you can imagine."

"I thought we were going to stay with you."

"In a way, yes. I too live in the boarding house, in a separate part of the same building. I guess they thought the clergyman could need some privacy now and then."

"Don't you have guest rooms?"

Luke glanced at Gillian, his eyes glistening with mirth over the sulking twelve-year-old in the back seat, and she rolled her eyes in response. Daisy was a force to be reckoned with, and when she got an idea in her head it was usually quite hard to get it out.

"I have a sofa bed."

"So why can't we stay there, with you? We won't disturb your privacy too much."

"Daisy!" Gillian turned and gave her daughter a pointed look. "You know better than to hassle someone who shows us kindness. The boarding house will be perfect for us, so please stop this unfit stubbornness now."

"But Mommy…!"

"No, Daisy. I mean it. Just stop it."

Daisy sank down in the back seat and crossed her arms, her lower lip thrust out in a pout. Luke didn't make a sound, but his shoulders trembled with laughter, and Gillian shook her head in frustration.

"You just wait, mister. One day you'll have a teenager too, and then you'll come crawling to me, begging me to forgive you for laughing."

"I wouldn't mind."

She snorted with fake disbelief. "You wouldn't

mind being a parent to a teenager? Man, you don't know what you are talking about."

"Not if that teenager would be as wonderful as Daisy. She seems to be just perfect."

"Perfectly stubborn," Gillian muttered between her teeth.

"I heard that!" Daisy called from the back seat, and Gillian exchanged an amused look with Luke.

"Daisy, that's enough. We're staying in the boarding house, and that's it. Now, let's just move into our new home, and hopefully I, your poor, exhausted mother, will be able to take another de-stressing, nerve-calming bath."

"You will not like this," Luke said as he stopped his car in front of his house, "but the boarding house rooms have only showers. Sorry about that. I hope you can survive."

"Oh, no." Gillian made an overly shocked face which had Luke smiling. "How will I ever survive without being able to soak my problems away?"

Daisy, who didn't have time to patiently sit and wait for the grownups to stop talking, bounced out of the car and disappeared into the lush garden, exploring her new surroundings.

"You are welcome to use both my tub and my sofa bed if you want to."

There it was. She closed her eyes for a second, trying to find the right words. Gillian took a deep breath, guessing this was a moment as good as any.

"Thank you, but I can't stay with you, Luke."

Chapter Nine

Sensing her seriousness, Luke turned slightly toward her, offering her his whole attention. "Why not? Is it because of me?"

"No, Luke. Not because of you. It's all because of me." She made an uncomfortable grimace, trying to find the right words to explain everything without hurting his feelings. At least not too much. "I was so much in love with you before I left Barnesville, so I kind of expected to feel the same about you when I returned. I'm afraid I pushed forward too fast and too much just because of what I used to feel and not what I feel for you now, for the person you are now."

His unreadable eyes held her pinned, and she squirmed uncomfortably under his gaze, not knowing how to proceed. She hadn't a clue to how he received her shaky confession.

"That's why I can't, even though it might be just for a while," she continued before completely losing her stamina. "I'm not staying, Luke. I will be going back home in a few weeks' time, and when my mother passes away I will only come back to pack her things and put up for sale whatever she has left me. We have a life somewhere else, a good life. Moving would mean losing my job, the only security we have, and Daisy would lose her school and friends."

Still staring silently at her, Luke didn't give

anything away, and Gillian was getting annoyed with him. He could at least let her know his thoughts and feelings about what she'd just told him.

"I think you must agree with me that the boarding house is the best solution."

She put her hand on the door handle but stopped when she heard his hoarse voice.

"Wait."

She looked back at him, watching him run his fingers through his dark hair. He looked confused, as if he didn't really know what to think—a state of mind she could relate to. Too often, unfortunately.

"I have a confession to make," he said cautiously, seeming somewhat embarrassed. "I think I most unwittingly might have tricked you into thinking I want you."

That certainly wasn't what she had thought he was going to say. Speechless, she stared at him, not knowing what to say. *He* had tricked *her*? Hadn't she just admitted to the other way around, that it was *she* who had tricked *him*?

"You dazzled me when we met the other day, you know. It was like a blast from the past because you made me feel like eighteen again. But yesterday, after we were interrupted by news of the accident, it bugged me that I didn't feel frustrated about the intrusion. Instead I felt almost relieved. It didn't take me too long to figure out that even though I like you a lot, I'm just not attracted to you. Oh, don't look so upset, you *are* a very attractive woman. But you are just not the woman I want."

She should be upset, Gillian thought, watching him squirm after throwing the truth in her face, but she wasn't. Not after listening to Candice tell what she felt for this man and how she had thought Gillian's arrival ended their budding romance.

"I hope I haven't destroyed anything between us because of my honesty." His earnest eyes begged her for forgiveness. "I still need you as my friend, Gillian. I-I don't know if it's just me, but…" Again he ran his fingers through his hair, as he had always done when feeling uneasy and insecure. "You and me, we have something between us, something that makes me so damn comfortable around you. It feels as if I can talk to you about everything, and considering I am a man who talks mostly just about sports and barbecuing, with everyone else…"

She couldn't help but laugh over his brutal honesty. Oh, she felt a little torn over being so easily discarded, but then again… Listening to what he said about them, about the strange bond between them, she knew he was right. There was something between them that made her feel at home.

Not as she felt when she was with Andrew; that was a completely different sensation. He was the man who made her whole body come alive, made her heart sing with excitement and her soul relax.

With Luke it was more a silent affection, almost sisterly in its simplicity. She felt at ease with him, and as a teenager she must have confused those feelings for love, because she didn't know how it felt to be loved or to be in love.

"No hard feelings?"

His strangled voice cut through her thoughts, and she shook her head, smiling. "No hard feelings whatsoever. As a matter of fact, I am almost relieved, too, and perhaps just a tad annoyed with myself for not seeing this earlier."

He smiled his crooked smile and held out his arms to her. With a contented sigh, she moved closer to him in the car and leaned into his embrace.

"So now you'll stay with me?" he asked into her hair and she nodded, hitting his chin with her forehead.

"Ouch... No, we won't. Think about the gossip. The tongues would never stop wagging if I did sleep over at your place, even with Daisy as company. But I will accept your generous offer of the tub, and I promise not to be too selfish with it."

She leaned back again, and his grin had deepened even more as he looked at her with a question in his eyes? "Selfish?"

"Well, you are a bachelor who willingly, perhaps stupidly, is letting two women into his silent home. One is a very loud, very outspoken almost-teenager who will not let your head rest for more than a few minutes when she's around."

"Sounds like heaven."

"Stupidly, then." His laughter followed her as she got out of the car and, with her gaze, tried to find her elusive daughter.

"Are we moving in?" Daisy called out as she reappeared from behind a lovely rosebush, and Gillian shook her head.

"Not with Luke, but we can use his tub."

As Luke came up beside her carrying two suitcases, he watched the sour-faced Daisy cartwheel all over the lawn. "I think she liked the thought of you two staying with me."

"You *think*?" Gillian laughed, grabbing the last

suitcase and following him to the door. "Well, I guess that is a mother's job, to disappoint the children now and then so they don't get too shocked when they grow up."

The two guestrooms Luke took them to in the rectory were gorgeous—two old-fashioned rooms with one large four-poster bed in each taking up most of the floor space. Daisy couldn't hide her excitement and started to squeal with delight with every new detail of the lovely old boarding house, and Gillian quickly forbade all gymnastics moves indoors before her daughter could continue cartwheels or anything else.

Back in Luke's rooms, as he had kindly offered to make them lunch, Gillian looked around curiously. The first time she had been here, the other day, she had been too occupied with Luke to notice anything but him, but now she explored both the room Luke used as a combined living room/dining room and the adjoining bedroom, opening all the doors she could find.

"You're snooping," Luke called out from the small kitchen pantry where he and the still-bouncing Daisy fixed lunch.

"I know," she called back, diving into his bedroom, admiring the old wooden furniture. She smiled when she noticed the dirty clothes lying forgotten on the floor next to the bed, and she couldn't stop herself from teasing him. "You forgot your laundry!"

"Are you in *my* room?"

"Yup."

Two seconds later, Luke dashed into the room and grabbed the laundry, throwing it into the laundry hamper standing by the door. "Sorry about that. When I left this morning, I didn't know I would have a snooper here later in the day."

"Don't you remember what we learned when we were scouts? Be prepared."

"I have Mrs. Cooper; I don't need to be prepared. There is nothing to prepare myself for."

"Oh, no? If I remember correctly, I was here yesterday, as I am here now, and as far as I know I still haven't met your watchdog. Is she forgetting to man her post?"

"You will meet up with her sooner or later. She's probably in the other part of the house taking care of all the guests. I won't hold it against you if you decide to move somewhere else once you have run into her. She can be a bit"—he held his chin, in a dramatically thoughtful pose, and Gillian giggled—"interfering, one could say."

She went to a large painting hanging on one wall, almost covering it completely. It was fascinating, with open stormy ocean and a ship facing a wave two times higher than itself. "Why don't you just tell her to leave, then? I don't think she'd think too badly of you for wanting your own life back."

"Oh, no, I can't do that. She would be completely devastated. I know, because she just told me the other day how lucky she thought herself to be, finding this job to go to, as she has no family of her own to take care of now that her husband died last year. She even suggested she could move here, into one of the bedrooms you and Daisy will have, to make sure I had everything I needed."

"Lucky for me, then, that you told her no."

"Uh…"

Her laughter was refreshingly honest, from deep

down inside her, shaking her body as she laughed until her belly muscles ached.

"You haven't told her no?"

"I tried," Luke whined. "She wouldn't listen."

"Oh, this is absolutely fabulous. I can hardly wait for her to show up, to see her face when you tell her the spare rooms are now occupied."

"You will not be there when I tell her about you two moving in. She will be unhappy, I'm sure, and it would be too cruel of me to let you stay and watch her suffer."

"Oh, come on, Luke. You really think she will suffer? She's an older lady with a life of her own and a will we all had to surrender to, once upon a time. I don't think she will take it as badly as you seem to. She might be a bit disappointed, but still..." Gillian paused, watching Luke squirm. He was so much fun to tease, such an easy target. "I hardly think she will throw a large tantrum just because you haven't a room available for her. And, let's face it, now you have shown how willing you are to fill your home with people, she will probably think it much easier to persuade you to accept her presence as soon as Daisy and I have left."

He actually blanched, and she couldn't hold back a hoot of laughter, completely destroying the truthfulness of her tale.

"You toad," he said between his teeth, giving her a look meant to kill. "Don't you ever do something like that to me again. I'm suffering here, you know. Mrs. Cooper is one of the nicest people I know. I don't want her to be unnecessarily upset."

"You'll live," Gillian said cheerfully as she passed him on her way out of his room, heading back toward the kitchen.

"Of course I'll live," he mumbled behind her. "I'll just be alone and miserable for the rest of my life because she'll probably set out to destroy my happiness completely. You know, the whole *if I can't have him, no one else will either* thing."

A foul stench of burning met their noses as they entered the kitchen, and Luke swore. With an anguished groan he dumped the frying pan with its now blackened contents into the sink, sighing heavily as he looked at the remains of what had been a very promising lunch.

"Damn."

"My sentiment exactly," Gillian agreed solemnly, moving to his side so she could look down into the sink. "It used to smell delicious."

"Sandwich?"

It was the best lunch she'd ever had, eating bologna sandwiches with Luke and Daisy in the cozy kitchen of the rectory. Luke could be hysterically funny when he wanted, and now he used every last drop of it. Daisy looked like a fish out of water, gasping for air because she was laughing so hard.

Gillian couldn't stop smiling as she watched the two of them engage in a crazy word battle neither of them could win but both refused to lose. Their dark-haired heads leaned closer and closer until their foreheads almost touched, and Gillian caught herself wishing Luke was the one.

That Luke was the father of her child.

There was no other likeness between them, but then again, Daisy was the spitting image of her mother and grandmother. The only difference was the dark hair, which looked so much the same shade as Luke's.

Daisy, who hadn't thought about anything but finding her elusive father when they arrived, seemed to have put the search on ice the last couple of days and instead spent all her time with her newfound friends. But Gillian knew her daughter—she wouldn't forget.

So maybe Gillian should continue the hunt? Maybe she should spill a question here and there, forcing her former friends to talk about the senior prom. Maybe she could find a person who had seen her with someone.

"I'm off to Annie's," Daisy said as she put her dishes away in the dishwasher. "We are going to go prince-hunting among the frogs of Oak Lane Pond. And no, I can't promise not to fall into the pond, but I'll try not to."

"Daisy…"

"Love you!" And with a quick peck on her mother's nose Daisy disappeared out through the door, a content twelve-year-old on the verge of becoming a teenager.

"She's adorable," Luke said, watching the girl through the window as she ran across the lawn toward her friend's house. "You must be so proud."

"I am."

"And her father? Is he in the picture? Neither of you speak of him, so one can't help but wonder…"

"There is no father to speak of, I'm afraid. He disappeared long before she was born. It's been only the two of us all these years."

Compassionately Luke grabbed her slender hands in his larger ones. "I'm so sorry to hear that. Both of you deserve a loving man in your lives."

"Deserve?"

"Yup." He grinned impishly. "I think every good

woman deserves a loving man."

"And I used to wonder why you still remained a bachelor…"

"I've been married a long time, babe. First to my big ego and then to the good Lord. There hasn't been a place in my life for a wife until now."

"But *now* you're searching for someone?"

He blushed slightly, and she bit back her smile, amused that she knew what his secret was and he hadn't a clue about it.

"Not actively. Too many other things to do. But I might have one special woman in mind that I have a good feeling about and who I think would fit me perfectly."

"Is it someone I know?" she asked, fully aware the answer was a loud yes. After all, Candice had been and hopefully still remained one of her very best friends.

"N-no," he stuttered, and she gave him a patronizing smile to show him she didn't believe a word he said. To tease him a bit more, she held up her hand in front of her, pretending great interest in her nails.

"I must admit I'm a bit envious. There's so much love in the air here in Barnesville. I mean, here you sit, confiding about finding someone to love, and earlier today, at the diner, Candy did the same. I can't tell you how glad I am that the two of you have each found someone special to you, because if anyone deserves to be happy, it's the two of you."

"Oh, she did, now, did she?" Luke's eyes started to glisten, and his crooked smile warmed her as he caught her game.

"Candy couldn't stop talking about him, you know,

told me all about him. Sounded like a really dull guy."

"Dull, you say?"

She nodded, still managing to keep her serious face on. "Dullest there is. But hey, who am I to have an opinion about the man she decides to give her heart to? From her description, I don't know this one personally, so I guess I'll have to meet him first."

Luke leaned back in the kitchen chair, his eyes laughing at her. "I guess you don't know everybody here in Barnesville anymore. You have, after all, been away for many years, and there have actually been some daredevils who have moved in here—by their own will, mind you."

"Really? Poor souls."

"Oh, I think they thought it absolutely picture perfect at first, especially considering our own welcoming committee greeting them with apple pie and a false impression of being friendly."

"Sally Barnes." Gillian shook her head. "We must be thankful, then, that Candy's boyfriend managed to survive such an attack and stayed on. She does sound like she's starting to fall for the guy."

"Starting, you say? I would rather say she's very much into him."

"Oh, she was, but then he met some old flimsy from yesteryear and started to follow her around, ignoring poor Candy, so now she's not so positive anymore."

A frown marred his forehead as he scowled at her, not liking the picture she was painting of him. "I never thought about Candy's feelings. Do you think she can forgive me?"

Gillian shrugged lightly. "I honestly don't know,

Luke. You haven't been very attentive to her lately, and I'm sorry to say that a woman scorned..."

"I have to go," Luke said, looking both determined and frightened as he stood up. "It seems I'd better head down to the diner before she decides I'm not worth her time."

"You'd better."

He grinned again. "Thanks, Gillian. Please, make yourself even more at home than you already have, if you can, and don't hesitate to continue the snooping."

"Oh, I will, don't you worry. And I most definitely will use that enormous bath of yours."

"I had a feeling you would." And with one last crooked smile, he vanished through the door. Only moments later she heard his car drive away.

Men! She gave a wry smile. *The diner is a five-minute walk away, and he still takes the car.*

After cleaning the kitchen, she continued her sightseeing throughout the wonderful old house, straightening a painting here, plumping a pillow there. She met a lot of the people who lived in the boarding house, most unknown to her previously, but the infamous Mrs. Cooper was nowhere to be seen.

When she came back to Luke's part of the house, she walked into the spacious bathroom with its enormous bathtub. Looking down into it, she knew exactly how she would spend the next hour of her day before she had to go back to her mother's house and let her and her friends bully her—she would take another bath.

The bathroom cabinet was filled with different oils and bath salts, and it was easy to tell Luke too enjoyed soaking. While the water slowly filled the tub, she lit the purple candles standing on a shelf, and soon a faint scent of lavender surrounded her.

"Ah…" She groaned with pleasure as she lowered her body into the inviting water and leaned her head back against the rolled towel she'd put on the edge of the tub as a pillow. She closed her eyes.

This was heaven.

The warmth of the water and the relaxing air in the rectory had her heart feeling light and easy. Moving out of her mother's house had been the best decision she'd made since arriving to Barnesville. For the last couple of weeks she had suffered while staying in her childhood home, haunted by old memories.

She would never be able to thank Luke enough for his generosity. To open up his home, and bathtub, for them had been a Samaritan act of kindness; to her it was a saving grace.

Sleepiness overtook her and with a contented sigh she let her thoughts drift away. Soon the world around her disappeared as she drifted into dreamland.

"Luke!"

A voice penetrated her lovely dreams, and drowsily she opened her eyes slowly. The lukewarm water and her raisin-like fingertips told her she had slept in the comfortable tub for a long time, maybe too long. With a groan she sat up, reaching for her wristwatch, and groaned again as she realized just how long she had slept.

"Where are you, my man?"

Oh, dear Lord! Gillian gasped as she recognized the smooth voice. Hastily she stood and reached for a towel, just as the door flew open and a man came barging into the bathroom.

Andrew.

He stopped midstride when he saw her standing in the tub with water up to her knees and a small towel pressed against her naked body. At first he just blinked, his mouth open in shock as he took in the picture in front of him.

"Gilly?" His voice was hoarse as he took a step toward her, warming her with his growing smile. "I didn't know you were here…"

His gaze was focused on the small hand towel that didn't cover much more than her most private parts, and she shivered as his gaze followed the length of her legs. The warmth in his eyes grew hotter and hotter, and soon she felt as if she would burn up under his roaming look.

"Oh, God," she whispered, trying to make herself as small as possible behind her towel.

He lifted his hot gaze to her face, and her knees grew weak.

"I have looked for you all day." His voice was low and smooth, and she shivered even more in delightful response. "I came here to ask Luke if he knew your whereabouts, and instead I find you…" His voice trailed off as he realized the meaning of what he'd just said. All the warmth he'd shown vanished, and something cold filled his blue eyes. "Why are you here?"

His clipped voice made her shiver just as much as his hot gaze had. "I moved here today."

A wry smile grew on his lips as he took a step backwards. "You? You living here? With…with Luke?"

"In the boarding house, yes. I-I had to get away

from Mother's house. I couldn't stand it, Andy. I had to get away."

"And so you went to *Luke*?"

The hurt in his voice was endless, and she held up a hand toward him. "Please, Andy, you have to understand. It was eating me up. You know how much I hate that house. To constantly be surrounded by Sally and her friends made me feel sick. I just had to get out of there. I had to get Daisy out of there."

"But why Luke? Why not…" He took a deep breath. "Why didn't you come to me?"

"It wasn't like that. I never meant to come here either. It was Candice who suggested I should move out of Mother's house to get some distance from Mother and her friends. She was the one who thought I should ask Luke about moving into the boarding house, and he was kind enough to offer us a room here."

"Of course he did."

"Andy…"

He shook his head, staggering backwards. "This is just too much. Oh, my God, Gilly. I-I didn't think you could hurt me more than you already have, and yet you still managed to find a new way."

"Andy…"

The sadness in his eyes was overwhelming. "Let's just stay friends, Gilly, like we always have been. You are not to blame for this. I'm the one who keeps throwing my hopes after you, refusing to believe in what you have been telling me all these years—it is Luke you want."

"That's not true! You are misunderstanding this," she cried out as he started out the door. "It's not what you think!"

He turned, looking more angry than she had ever seen him. "So this is not what I think, is it? Please do tell me, then, Miss Gillian Crane, what else can it be?"

She opened her mouth to convince him what she had just said was the truth, because she knew she couldn't live with him feeling this much disdain for her.

"What is going on here?"

A voice from the past interrupted the heated moment as Mrs. Cooper appeared in the doorway behind Andrew. "What are the two of you doing here in Lucas's house? And in his tub, of all places!"

"I was just searching for Luke, but it seems I'll have to find him elsewhere." Andrew ripped his gaze from Gillian and turned around to walk past their old teacher. "Lookin' good, Mrs. C."

"Andy, please don't leave."

Ignoring Gillian's heartfelt plea, Andrew left the bathroom without looking back. Tears filled her eyes. She knew she had spoiled the one chance she'd had for true love.

Her one shot at happiness.

Chapter Ten

"You look like you could use a cup of coffee." Mrs. Cooper peered at Gillian, who had just come into Luke's small kitchen after putting on some clothes.

"Thank you. That would be lovely."

As the older woman rummaged around in the kitchen cabinets, Gillian watched her old teacher, amazed at how she still looked the same as she had years ago. Her thin gray hair was wrapped into the same tight little bun, and the smooth skin of her face was amazingly unwrinkled for her age. She still wore the same kind of flowery dress under a thin cardigan, and her small feet were enclosed in the same kind of practical shoes Gillian remembered.

"I'm so embarrassed," Gillian admitted. She had to at least try to explain what had happened, why she had been in Luke's bathtub, and the presence of Andrew.

"Why?" Mrs. Cooper's eyes danced with mirth. "If anyone should be embarrassed, it should be me, who didn't understand I was intruding until it was too late. But I have to admit I do wonder what you are doing here."

"When Luke heard my daughter and I were looking for somewhere to stay, he kindly offered us two of the guest rooms until we are ready to leave town."

"Did he, now?"

"Uh…yes…"

"Well, I'm not surprised." Mrs. Cooper held out a basket of muffins, surprising Gillian with her kind, almost proud smile. "Lucas is such a sweetheart. Of course he wouldn't want you to stay anywhere else."

After hearing all about Mrs. Cooper being such a resentful watchdog, it was heartening to listen to the woman's belief in her employer. Especially considering she'd had to endure him at school once upon a time when he hadn't been the best-behaved child.

As she nibbled on a muffin, Gillian felt less aggravated. Again the coziness of the kitchen took over, calming her, while Mrs. Cooper's familiar face and understanding attitude soothed her tattered nerves.

The feeling didn't last long, though; she had completely forgotten about her old teacher's infamous straightforwardness.

"So, Gillian dear, what else can it be?"

"Excuse me?"

"What dear Doctor Marshall asked you in the bathroom, you know, when you stood there almost as naked as the day you were born—and I should know, since I was the midwife's helper back then and the first person to hold you."

The simple admission, sewn into the more intricate question, took Gillian back for a moment. "You were there when I was born?"

"Indeed I was. I saw and held most of you youngsters in my arms the day you blessed the world with arriving."

She hadn't known that, Gillian realized, and it became clearer and clearer to her how her mother was a clam when it came to anything but her charities and the daily chores. So many things Gillian had never known, simple things which didn't mean anything to anyone but her, such as what Mrs. Cooper now told her.

"But enough about that now," Mrs. Cooper said as she sat down facing Gillian. "What else can it be?"

Gillian sighed. She had known Mrs. Cooper all her life and felt the utmost respect for her. Just as when she had talked to Alma the other day, she knew she didn't want to lie. Not to the ones who actually did care for her. She'd never had any problem lying to her mother, though, which said more about her mother than it did about her.

"Andy was just a bit upset about me staying here at the rectory. That's all."

"Now, why would a levelheaded man like Andrew Marshall become upset over such a thing? It's not uncommon for the minister of this town to help the ones in need of a bed by offering them room in the boarding house."

"Because he thinks I'm about to sleep in Luke's bedroom instead of in one of the guest rooms."

Mrs. Cooper frowned slightly. "Why would you sleep in Luke's bedroom when there's a perfectly suitable guest room for you to…"

When Gillian arched her eyebrows pointedly, Mrs. Cooper's voice trailed off, and she lost all her color. "Oh. Well, that wouldn't do, now, would it?"

Gillian had problems following her train of thought. "Why wouldn't that do?"

"Uh…it makes Doctor Marshall upset."

Mrs. Cooper's face had regained some color, but she didn't mention what had shocked her so. Instead she sipped her coffee, staring absentmindedly out into space.

Gillian leaned back, sighing with frustration. What was wrong with the people of this town? What had happened that had made them so eager to overlook the fact that Andrew was married and urge her to pursue him into infidelity?

She looked at Mrs. Cooper, across the table from her, and knew there was no one better to ask. As far as she knew, her old teacher had never lied to her. At least she never used to.

"Why would it make Andy upset?"

Mrs. Cooper turned a startled gaze on her before regaining her wits. "Because he loves you, of course. I thought you knew that."

Again the same naturalness as everyone else seemed to have regarding Andrew cheating on his wife.

Gillian was getting a bit annoyed with that attitude. "Really, Mrs. Cooper? You think it's okay for Andy to love me? To want me? To get upset over the thought of me sleeping with another man? Why?"

"Aren't you overdoing it a bit now, Gillian? What is wrong with someone loving you? You should be grateful instead of annoyed. You can never get too much love in your lifetime."

Ignoring the last part, Gillian yelled, "*His wife*!"

"Who?"

Gillian threw out her hands in despair. "Oh, come on. What's the matter with the people of this town? Why does everyone seem to think it's okay for a married man to desire someone else? Even Andrew does, and I would never have thought he would be so disrespectful toward marriage, especially his own."

"You think Andrew's married?" Mrs. Cooper's chin dropped in shock for a moment, but finally her eyes twinkled with mirth and a hoarse laugh erupted from somewhere deep inside her as if it had been hiding away there for years and only now unleashed. "Oh, this is hilarious. Poor man! No wonder he has looked like the Ghost of Christmas Past ever since you got back to town."

"I *know* he's married. He told me as much himself."

"Did he, now? That's strange, considering he isn't married and, as far as I know, has never considered it at all, much to his mother's frustration. That is, I might add, not until you returned."

Gillian sat back, watching Mrs. Cooper dry her eyes on a lacy handkerchief, still shaking her head, now and then still letting out a small burst of laughter.

She really didn't know what to think.

That first day, when she and Daisy had arrived in Barnesville and they had met Andrew, he had told her he was married. Or had he?

She ransacked her memory, trying to focus on that sweet moment outside the doctor's office when he had overwhelmed her with the man he had become. She had asked him if he had someone special in his life, and he had most definitely told her he had.

She had assumed he'd meant he was married, maybe because she hadn't thought it possible that someone as special as he was could still be unspoken for. But then again, he *had* told her he had someone special in his life. And as she thought about it, she remembered something else—it wasn't just Andrew who had talked about him being married.

"Mrs. Cooper, all my friends spoke about his wife in front of him, and Luke even told Andy to go home to his wife and cuddle with her. Now, why would Luke say something like that to Andy, who most certainly didn't deny it even though I stood there with them, listening?"

At this, Mrs. Cooper howled with laughter, banging her knees with her palms, her complexion changing to beet red. It wasn't so hard to figure out the woman found Gillian beyond hysterically funny, and Gillian was getting quite annoyed with her.

"What?" she barked as soon as Mrs. Cooper calmed down enough to listen to her. "What is it that is so funny?"

"The cat," Mrs. Cooper whispered breathlessly.

"Excuse me?"

"He named his cat 'Wife.' That's the one everyone meant. Not a woman. A cat."

Sinking back into the chair again, Gillian felt drained of both air and emotions.

A cat.

If she hadn't been too tired from all the emotional stress of the last couple of weeks, she would have joined Mrs. Cooper and laughed until tears ran down her cheeks too. But she couldn't.

A damn cat.

Closing her eyes, she thought about Andrew and what he had said and done when he was with her, and she couldn't agree more with Mrs. Cooper.

Poor man…

It amazed her he still had come for her today, considering how selfishly she had behaved toward him lately. Andrew didn't know she was acting under the mistaken impression that he was married. All he knew was that they were two available singles, free to do whatever they wanted with whomever they wanted.

Again and again, ever since she had arrived a little more than a week ago, he had opened up his arms and his heart for her, and every time she had walked all over him, refusing to listen to his quiet words of affection. And her ruthlessness didn't end there. No, she had repeatedly insisted on flaunting her old obsession with Luke in front of him, almost forcing Andrew to help her find a way for her to get together with the man of her dreams. Or at least the man she had dreamt about as a teenager.

"You have to talk to him." Mrs. Cooper, who finally had calmed herself down, sent her an amused look over her cup. "Alma says he's not been himself lately, which she thinks is quite odd, especially when knowing how eagerly he awaited your arrival after he heard you were coming home."

A lump grew in her throat and Gillian had to blink to force the telling tears away. "He did?"

"It's been quite hard for Alma to watch her wonderful son spend year in and year out waiting for you. Not that he ever said he was waiting. No, it was more the comments he made about all the women she threw in his way that gave away what he unconsciously was doing. There was always something wrong with them—you know, one was too brown-haired, another one too tall, and so on. It wasn't so hard to figure out he always compared them to the memory he had of you, and who can compete with a memory?"

"No one, not even the person in the memory," Gillian mumbled, too aware she had done the same thing in comparing everyone with the faint memory she'd had of Luke. And, to be completely honest, not even he had managed to live up to the image she'd had of him.

"Exactly. And that's why Alma took the matter into her own two capable hands and had the nurse call you."

Gillian nodded absentmindedly. Of course it hadn't been her mother who had sent for her. Her cold and unwelcoming air had said as much. Even when Gillian got the call she had somewhere deep inside of her known she still was unwanted and would only suffer if she went back. But the little girl she once had been had forced her to go and see if maybe…

Why had she returned to Barnesville?

Her mother had not only kicked her out, all those years ago, but she had forced Gillian to promise never to come back. Devastated by the whole situation, Gillian never had. She had locked away all thoughts and feelings linked to her hometown and had not let any of them come forward until the day the nurse called and told her that her dying mother wanted her by her side.

Overwhelmed by wave after wave of gratitude over finally being wanted and needed, she hadn't stopped to think twice about it. Instead, she had more or less thrown Daisy into the car and dragged her daughter into the lion's den.

"I don't think she ever expected to see him suffer as much as he has during the last couple of weeks. Oh, he hasn't said a word about it to her, but she's his mother—she knows."

"She must hate me."

"Of course she doesn't." Mrs. Cooper snorted. "She blames herself entirely. If she hadn't interfered, he might have reconsidered his chosen path in life. Men have biological clocks too, you know, and Andrew's has been ticking away quite loudly lately. Alma says she's seen a change in him toward the women he meets nowadays. He doesn't write them off immediately without giving them a chance."

"But why does Alma blame herself for opening up his eyes?" Gillian asked, intrigued even though the mere thought of Andrew meeting someone else hurt immensely. "I know how much she loves her children, and I can't think she would blame herself for acting the part of matchmaker for one of them."

"The thing is, Alma got too impatient. When Andrew showed every sign of being ready to move on in life and start a family of his own, she just couldn't sit still and wait for things to happen. She wants him to be happy, because he is such a dear boy and deserves all the love in the world. So at first she paraded every single woman she could find in front of him, searching for any sign that he saw something special in any one of them, but it was too soon. He wasn't ready to fall in love with anyone—he still had to get you out of his heart first. And that's when she decided the nurse should call you, because she knew without any doubt you would come home to Barnesville if your mother asked you to."

"And so I did."

"Indeed you did, and that's when everything went wrong, at least from Alma's point of view." Mrs. Cooper gave an amused chuckle. "Not only did you bump into Andrew first thing, and more or less knock him off his feet with your warmth and obvious affection for him, but then you also made it perfectly clear you were single."

"I never meant to imply…"

"Of course you didn't. Again, Gillian, this is not your fault. Andrew has this soft spot for you that's unyielding to anyone else, and all it took was one smile to bring back all those old emotions for him."

It was such a mess. An emotional tornado she never had yearned for but now was caught in the middle of. She had walked unbeknownst into the hornets' nest, and now all she could do was try to treat all the stings, one after another.

"It must have been so frustrating for Alma."

"Not at first. You see, she loves you dearly too, and when she realized her little ploy might have turned out even better than she had dared to dream about, that the two of you would end up together, she practically waltzed around on clouds."

"Until I hurt Andrew."

"Hurt is such a soft word." Mrs. Cooper's eyes twinkled. "Maul would be a better description. Over and over again, until the poor man turned into the pile of mincemeat he is today."

"And now it is too late," Gillian whispered to herself, thinking about how definite he had been when he left.

Let's just stay friends.

"It is never too late," Mrs. Cooper said cheerfully. "Go hunt the man down somewhere private and tell him what's in your heart."

"What if I don't know what's in my heart?"

"Do you love him?"

She nodded. "Yes, I think I do."

"You *think* you do? Either you do or you don't."

Again frustration took over and she threw out her

hands in despair. "Why do I have to know how I feel? This is all so new to me, loving Andrew."

"So you didn't love him before you left Barnesville?"

"Of course I did. I loved him more than I ever can express, he meant absolutely everything to me. But I didn't love him like a woman loves a man, back then. What I felt for him was a child's love, a sister's love. And that's what's confusing to me now, because it was so easy to feel more for the grownup Andrew, and I'm just not sure if…"

Mrs. Cooper's unreadable eyes looked at her as she sank back in the chair, lost for words. "You are not sure if what you feel is the same old sisterly love, or if it is a grown woman's love."

Gillian nodded, deflated. "I need time and space to figure things out, something he doesn't want to give me. And now it's over. You heard what he said to me in the bathroom. He wants us to stay friends from now on. Not lovers, friends."

"That's his hurting heart talking, dear. He's a man, and to a man everything is black or white. All those shades of gray just don't exist in their natural habitat. He thinks you want Luke, and because he loves you he will back off to give you what you want."

To Gillian's surprise, Mrs. Cooper's words actually did make sense, in a strange and roundabout way. Andrew was unknowingly giving her what she wanted, space to figure things out. But what scared her was the thought of him finding a new path in life before she'd had time to come to terms with what she wanted.

If she didn't talk to him about how she felt, would he wait for her? What if Andrew met someone else and, in his new loneliness, found that someone attractive enough to want to spend the rest of his life with her, without knowing Gillian was trying to work things out in her mind?

Then it really would be too late.

Yet speaking with Andrew and asking him to wait for her wasn't kind, either. Just thinking of staying in Barnesville, in this small-minded community, made her feel nauseous. She had nothing here.

Andrew, on the other hand, had his whole life here, both a loving family and a good job. She knew he would probably move away with her if she asked him to, but she would always know he did it only for her, not for himself. And she couldn't live with that, knowing he would forsake his needs and wants for hers, especially as she knew she would never do the same for him.

She hadn't worked so hard for the last decade, to get where she was today, just so she could throw it away on a whim and move in with Andrew and become Mrs. Doctor Marshall full time.

And then there was Daisy to consider. She too had a life back home, with a good school and many friends. It would be selfish to not at least consider what it meant for her almost-teenager to leave everything behind and move somewhere else.

"That was one deep sigh." Mrs. Cooper chuckled, and Gillian smiled sheepishly.

"I'm sorry. I'm just so confused, because even though I don't really know what I want, what I *do* know is that I don't want to lose Andrew before I know."

Another chuckle escaped Mrs. Cooper as Gillian rolled her eyes over her own tirade. "One step at time,

Gillian. One step at time. And if I were you, I would start with Andrew."

With determination written all over her face, Gillian grabbed her purse and headed for the door. "You are right. Please excuse me for leaving you like this, but I have somewhere I have to be. I'll see you later?"

"I'll be here."

Not until she stood outside the rectory did Gillian realize she hadn't a clue where he could have gone. He had said he was going to search for Luke, but that had just been a lie to fool the old teacher, she was sure. She looked down Main Street, toward the doctor's office, and when she couldn't see Andrew's old truck she decided to start at his home.

A blush crept over her cheeks as it dawned on her that she didn't know where he lived. Not once had she asked him where his house was located. The only thing she did know was that he didn't live at the farm anymore, with the rest of his family.

She guessed she could ask Alma, but then again, after hearing Mrs. Cooper's tale about how involved his mother had been in what had happened lately, she hesitated and instead decided to go to her mother's house. Rachel was, after all, a patient of his, and being the caring doctor he was, he visited her at least a couple of times every day, to see how she was doing in these last days of her life.

The old, enormous Victorian house lay quiet as she walked up to it, the windows staring dark and unwelcomingly at her. Andrew's truck was nowhere in sight, so he wasn't here, but the nurse would know if he would be coming anytime soon.

The house was just as silent as it had seemed from the outside, and when Gillian quietly entered her mother's bedroom, she found it almost empty—all the unfriendly friends gone with the wind.

"She sent them away, said they kept disturbing her sleep with their obnoxious care," the nurse enlightened her with a roll of her eyes, and Gillian bit back a smile. At least her mother still had her spunk.

"How is she doing?"

"Not well, I'm afraid. I just called Doctor Marshall and asked him to come by here as soon as possible. She seems to drift away now and then as if she's too tired to stay awake. And she also has started to cough a lot, something her heart has a hard time coping with."

After sending the nurse down to the kitchen to get something to eat, Gillian sat by her mother's bed, watching her sleep while waiting for Andrew to arrive. She followed every line of her mother's proud face with her eyes, desperately trying to memorize what she looked like.

Sadness over the deep cleft between them filled her heart, and tears ran down her cheeks. She knew it was silly, but somewhere deep inside of her the little girl she once had been still nourished a foolish wish that her mother would declare how much her daughter meant to her.

How much she loved her.

The adult Gillian knew this would never happen, but still…just once before she died…

"What are *you* doing here?"

Chapter Eleven

Looking up, Gillian met the cold, harsh gaze of her mother.

"I-I'm watching you wh-while Nurse Winters i-is eating," she stuttered, as if she had been caught doing something naughty when all she had done was sit quietly by her mother's bed.

"I thought I was rid of you."

Ignoring the pain in her heart, Gillian forced a strained smile, trying not to show her mother how much her words hurt. "Just because I've moved our things to the rectory doesn't mean I won't be…"

"Oh, my God!" her mother spit out, her voice twisted with agony. "You moved in with *him*? When will this shame ever end?"

"Wh-what?" Gillian stared openmouthed at her mother, not following her thoughts. "What's wrong with us staying at the rectory? Luke was just being helpful…"

"He's helped enough through the years, hasn't he? Not only has he fathered a child he not once has claimed as his own, thank God, but he also made sure my line will end with disgrace. *Disgrace!*"

One thing was quite clear: her mother thought Luke was Daisy's father, which wasn't so farfetched, since Gillian had been over the top crazy for him. Rachel wasn't the first person to come to that conclusion. Heck, Gillian too thought Luke was the most likely man for the position. But why was it a disgrace for them to stay at the rectory? If anything, she would have thought Rachel would think it the least of the worst. Socially, the boarding house was a perfectly acceptable hotel.

"I thought this was over, that I never would have to deal with it again. But you just had to come back, didn't you, and managed to do so when he too had returned. Oh, how I tried to get the others to send him away, to deny him the job as reverend, but in vain. They all thought him absolutely perfect. It seems only I can see what a swine he really is."

"Luke? Mother, what…"

"You never got it, did you? I knew I handled the whole affair wrongly when I didn't tell you the truth about him, the truth about who he is, especially as you thought yourself in love with him. But it was so obvious to everyone he wasn't feeling the same, and so, against my better judgment, I did not to admit my shame out loud. Oh, how I have regretted that decision!"

Her mother gasped for air after the tirade, and Gillian gave her the glass of water which stood on the nightstand, waiting impatiently while her mother emptied it. A faint feeling of hope rose up inside her as she almost hesitantly dared to believe she finally would be told why her mother hated her. Why she had sent her away, never to return, as soon as she found out Gillian was pregnant.

When she'd calmed down, Rachel gave Gillian the glass before sinking back into the pile of pillows, her hard gaze glued to her daughter's face.

"I'm right, aren't I? Lucas Walker is the father of your child?"

Your child, she said, not *my* granddaughter. Gillian felt her nostrils flare as she took a deep breath through her nose, forcing herself to not lash out toward her mother. This was not the moment to say exactly what she thought of her, not when Rachel finally seemed willing to open up and share what was in her heart.

"I don't know." The quiet answer surprised Rachel, and her scowl deepened.

"Of course you know who the father is. You were there when the child was conceived, weren't you?"

Taking another deep breath, Gillian tried to find some strength. She had never told anyone about senior prom night all those years ago, not until she'd spilled it all out to Daisy.

"I honestly don't know. I've tried to remember what happened, tried over and over again, but I was too drunk, and everything's just a blur."

"Drunk?" Rachel snorted disdainfully. "I guess we are speaking of that senior prom of yours, the one when the police came home with you throwing up in a bucket?"

"Yes. That one."

"Oh, I've never been more embarrassed in my life as I was when the sheriff had to carry your passed-out body up the stairs. Everyone could see what kind of daughter I had, a drunkard."

Her mother practically spit out the last word, leaving no doubt as to her feelings regarding what Gillian had done.

"Now you are being unfair," Gillian said as tears started to prick her eyes. "I'd never touched alcohol until the senior prom night, and I suspect that was why I got drunk so quickly."

"Someone probably spiked it. They always do, those rowdy boys, wanting the girls ripe for plucking."

Ignoring her mother's vile poison, Gillian closed her eyes, again trying to remember what had happened. "It was supposed to be the night I finally confessed my love for Luke, before we lost the closeness of school and continued out into the adult world. I remember Andrew came, looking so handsome in his father's suit, and he brought a corsage for my wrist."

The picture of the tall young man, awkward in his father's best suit, standing nervously on the porch with a slightly crushed corsage in his hand, came into her mind's eye. She smiled sadly, now knowing how important that night must have been to him, taking the girl of his heart to their senior prom.

But she had hardly noticed him or what he looked like. All she had thought about was Luke and how she had to do something before it was too late. Before he did what he always had talked about—leaving Barnesville.

"That poor boy," Rachel said with a faint, almost disdainful smile. "He couldn't stop staring at you in the fancy dress I had to buy you so you wouldn't disgrace me. He even called you an angel. But you didn't take time to notice his admiration. All you could talk about was Luke this and Luke that, and I was so glad it was all coming to an end, that finally we were going to get rid of the threat."

"Mother! How can you be so rude? There was nothing wrong with who Luke was back then. So what if he didn't come from the right side of town? He still was a good, hardworking young man and, furthermore, someone I, your own daughter, really cared for."

"There's nothing good with Lucas Walker! He took advantage of a drunken girl and knocked her up."

"Mother, please listen to me. I don't know if it was Luke. It could have been anyone. Heck, it could have been the sheriff, for all I know."

"Of course it was Lucas Walker. Who else would you have given in so easily to, not once considering the disgrace and embarrassment you dragged me through with your actions. Thank God no one knows the whole truth! I would have been devastated if someone found out what your child really is."

"Daisy. Her name is Daisy, not 'child,' and she's the most wonderful little girl there is, which you would know if you just looked at her, just talked to her."

"You are lucky," her mother scoffed, not listening to a word Gillian said. "Most inbreeds are retarded and mentally incapable."

"Inbreeds?" Gillian put a shaking hand to her mouth, trying to get a grip on what her mother was talking about. "Daisy is no inbreed."

"You really don't know?" Rachel sneered. "Your father, who everyone always talks so endearingly about, was just as big a disgrace to me as you were. Always chasing around after women, unrestrainedly flirting with anyone in a skirt. Your Lucas is the outcome of one especially messy affair he had with some young floozy."

Rachel's face was twisted with hatred, and Gillian shrank back even more, not knowing what to say or what to think. It couldn't be, could it? Could Daisy, her lovely, intelligent little daughter, be the child of two siblings?

"You must be mistaken. H-he can't be…"

"He is," Rachel interrupted icily. "And you know what? When your father learned the floozy was pregnant, he wanted to leave me. For her. He even begged me to divorce him, promised me anything as long as I agreed to separate. Of course I wouldn't. The scandal would have been too much. As the months passed and the child grew in his little friend's womb, he never ceased to nag and nag about it, even asked me if I didn't want to be happy and find someone who loved me. In the end I had no choice. One evening when he sat in his office drinking himself into a stupor as he always did every night by that time, I made sure he wouldn't leave me. I made sure I too got pregnant."

With me, Gillian thought, her heart crying for her father, who had found love too late and was caught in an arranged marriage he never asked for to a woman who was made of ice. No wonder her mother never had loved her. She had just been a pawn in her mother's plan to stay out of scandal's way.

"Wh-what happened to the young girl who was pregnant?" Gillian asked, her heart crying for the innocent caught in the middle of it all. "Why didn't she keep Luke?"

Rachel shrugged indifferently. "She never had a choice. When Henry learned I was pregnant with his child, he did whatever I asked, and so I made sure the baby was taken from her and given to a couple who wanted it. She fussed a bit at first, but when told she would lose her job, too, if she continued being stubborn about keeping the baby herself, and without a job she wouldn't be able to support her child anyway, she gave in. She had no money, and I made sure she had no friends. It was easy."

"Oh, Mother," Gillian cried, unable to believe Rachel's heartlessness, but her mother just snorted.

"You are so much like your father, Gillian, just as softhearted and weepy. If you hadn't had my looks, I would have thought you too came from another woman's womb. Stop feeling sorry for that woman. She could have had more children if she had wanted to, but she decided to remain unmarried. If she feels lonely, it's her own fault."

"B-but…"

"You can leave me now. Maybe now you will respect my wish to never see you or your child again. I don't want to spend my last days on earth constantly reminded of the shame you are to me, what you've put me through, you and your father."

Unable to move, Gillian stared at her mother in shock over what she had heard. The story was ugly and wrong from the beginning to the bitter end, and all because of the selfish woman in front of her. To Rachel it was all about who you were and where you came from. No wonder Gillian had never been able to please her and make her proud. It was an impossible mission.

And then she had committed the ultimate sin—she had become pregnant while unmarried, and the father was probably her half-brother.

With one last lingering look filled with contempt, Rachel turned her back toward her daughter, dismissing her from her mind and her life. Numbly Gillian stood up, hesitating slightly as there still was so much she wanted to say to this woman, but she couldn't find the right words.

In the end, she left the bedroom quietly, knowing there was nothing she could say. There were no words that would force Rachel to listen to her. In her mother's head she was born out of necessity and had been merely endured ever since. It must have been so frustrating to her mother that her father had died just a couple of years later, leaving her with a child she'd never wanted in the first place.

After informing the nurse her mother was by herself, she walked out through the door of her childhood home, knowing in her heart she would never return. All her life she had hated that house and what it represented, and now, when her mother finally had cut her free, she didn't want to go there again.

Slowly she walked down the street toward the church, dreading to confront Luke about what she had just learned. But there was no way round it. She had to know, for Daisy's sake, if he was the one she'd had sex with on senior prom night.

Because if it had been he…

The whole world turned upside down, and suddenly she was on her hands and knees by a bush as the luncheon she'd eaten earlier came back up.

As the retching eased, she crawled a few feet away before sinking down into the grass, her whole being screaming silently in mental agony.

Her beautiful daughter.

Her lovely, intelligent little girl.

What if Luke was her father? What would that do to Daisy and her future? Sooner or later Gillian would have to tell her, destroying her daughter's every chance of happiness. Because she had to tell her. She couldn't let her daughter walk out into the world the way her own mother had let Gillian unknowingly walk into the arms of her half-brother.

"Oh, my God, Gillian, are you hurt?" Andrew's frightened voice cut through her chaotic mind just as she felt his large hands grabbing hold of her head, steadying it. "Lie still, honey. If it was a car that hit you, it could be a concussion. Are you in pain?"

She tried to shake her head, but he held it steady, refusing to let go.

"I'm not hurt," she whispered and had to repeat the answer two more times before the message got through his frenzy and he reluctantly let go of her.

"When I saw you lying there…" Andrew's voice broke, and she could see how he struggled with the panic he had felt.

He helped her up until she stood beside him on shivering legs. She grabbed his arm hard, not able to let go just yet. No matter what would happen between them in the future, he still was the pole around which her whole world rotated, and just touching him made her feel stronger. It was amazing, really, how she had arrived here remembering him as her most beloved friend and now, a couple of weeks later, she didn't know how she ever would manage to live without him.

But she had to. If Luke was Daisy's father…

Nausea grabbed hold of her again, but this time she had nothing left to throw up and ended up in Andrew's loving embrace, her body shaking beyond her ability to control it.

"There, there," he mumbled into her hair, and she pressed her cheek against his chest, letting his steady heartbeat calm her. "Are you feeling better?"

She smiled reassuringly, which he couldn't see, as

Jennifer Wenn

she had her nose pressed into his jacket, so she nodded too, succeeding in bumping his chin with the top of her head. She couldn't stifle a laugh as he groaned softly into her hair.

"Ouch, that hurt."

"Sorry."

"You scared me."

She pressed herself closer to him. "I'm so sorry. I didn't think about where I was. I just lost it."

He let go of her waist and grabbed her chin instead, forcing her to lean backwards so he could look into her eyes. "What happened? And don't you think about not telling me. You know how much you mean to me, and seeing you like this... Well, let's just say I almost had to go home and change my pants."

She sighed, knowing in her heart he was right. But then again, she had to talk to Luke first. He was such a big part of this that he needed to have a say about this.

"I promise you I will tell you in time, but not now. Please, Andrew, believe me when I say I wouldn't have hesitated for a second if this was all about me. But I have to talk to Luke first. This is his problem as much as mine, and I just can't..."

She felt him withdraw from her, and tears sprang to her tired eyes as she saw his empty gaze staring back at her.

"Always Luke," he whispered as he let go of her, backing away from her.

"It's not what you think..." she began, but he interrupted her with a harsh laugh.

"You keep saying that, and I still don't believe you. It's exactly what I think."

He turned, walked briskly back to his truck, and

140

drove away without looking back.

So be it.

She had no fight left in her. If Andrew wouldn't believe her or have patience enough to wait for the truth as she asked him to, then she would have to deal with him later. And if later happened to be too late, then she had to live with it. She was used to putting her own needs aside, and as long as Daisy lived at home she could concentrate on her daughter. What would happen the day Daisy left home for college or wherever life took her was a whole different story. But for now it was enough.

Andrew had to wait.

As she continued on the short walk to the church, followed by curious eyes from the neighboring houses, she tucked the thoughts about Andrew away and instead pondered what to say to Luke. Not only was she going to have to tell him about their joint father, but she also had to ask him straight out if he had been the one at the senior prom. She had to ask him if he, her brother, was father to her daughter.

She had to wait until another attack of nausea eased before entering the rectory. Neither Luke nor Mrs. Cooper was anywhere to be seen, so she continued to the church.

Luke was standing in front of the altar, laughing with a group of children who stared just as starry-eyed at him as their teacher did. Looking at him with new eyes, Gillian found the family resemblance between him and their father was easy to see. Luke had the same straight nose as Henry had possessed, and the same square jaw and thick eyebrows that almost every man in the Crane family had been blessed with in the last five generations. The only difference was the same as between her and Daisy: Luke was just as dark-haired as Henry and the rest of the Cranes had been blond.

Luke's mother must have had dark hair, and maybe she was the one who had given him the crooked smile, too. Again she sent a sad thought to the woman who had been forced to give up not only the man she loved but their child too.

"Feeling a bit churchy today?" Luke walked up to her with a grin, and all of a sudden she realized this was her brother. Her sibling. All her childhood she had desperately wished for a sister or brother, someone to join forces with against their mother.

"What is it, Gillian?" Luke lost his smile as he noticed her pale face and shivering lips. "You look like you've seen a ghost."

"I talked to my mother today."

"Oh. That would do it, I guess." Luke's grin returned, but she was too nervous to smile with him.

"I need to talk to you in private."

He cast an eye on the pretty teacher who stood surrounded by her students by the altar, staring with a little too much interest at them, and with a wry grin he nodded toward the back door of the church. "Why don't we go to the vestry? We'll be alone there."

As the door closed behind them, Luke moved over to a small sofa, provided as a place where the clergyman could rest when he needed a minute or two for himself, and patted the seat next to him, inviting her to join him.

"So what was it Rachel said to you that has you running here in desperate need of resolution?" Luke tried to joke and, unbeknownst, gave Gillian the opening she had sought.

"She told me about your parents."

"My parents? What about them? They have been deceased for over a decade now. Both died in a car accident shortly after I enlisted."

Gillian shook her head. "Not the Walkers. I mean your real parents. The biological ones."

He froze, staring at her with unreadable eyes, and she sat silent, waiting for the questions which would come as soon as he sorted his thoughts.

"I don't understand," he finally let out, after staying silent for a long time. "How can your mother know anything about my biological parents? No one else knows anything. The records were destroyed when the old City Hall burned down. I know, because I've been at the new one, asking for them."

"Well, you see, my mother knows of your parents. As a matter of fact, she was the sole reason you were given away for adoption in the first place. Or, to be completely honest, *I* was."

Luke looked more and more confused at every word she said, and she couldn't blame him; it was a mess for her, too.

"You see," she said nervously, "Henry Crane, my father, is your father too."

Without moving a muscle, Luke stared into infinity, not showing at all what went on under that dark hair of his, and Gillian seized the opportunity to spit it all out. She told him about her father, and how he'd had a girlfriend on the side who got pregnant, and his request for a divorce. She let him know exactly what Rachel had said about her part in the whole thing, and how she had managed to not only keep her husband but also forever destroy happiness for the other woman and the love child—Luke.

When everything was said, she sat back on the sofa, waiting for his reaction. Luke didn't move. Silently he leaned forward, resting his elbows against his knees while staring absentmindedly at his hands. Not until a hard knock on the door echoed in the small chamber did he wake from his stupor.

"I guess I'd better see who it is," he mumbled, looking almost dizzy as he went to the door and opened it to face the pretty young teacher.

"I was just wondering if you could answer a few questions for the children," the teacher said with a pretty, flirtatious smile which it was quite clear Luke didn't notice, as he scowled at her.

"What? Yes, of course. I'll come with you." He went out into the hallway, following the swinging hips of the teacher, before halting abruptly.

"Stay," he said over his shoulder, his face as cold as his clipped voice, and Gillian nodded in response.

"I'll wait for you."

It took two hours before he returned, and by then Gillian was practically climbing the walls with fear. She knew she was behaving irrationally, but she was so used to being blamed for everything by her mother she just couldn't focus on the good side.

"I'm sorry you had to wait for so long," he apologized quietly when he returned, carrying two cups of steaming hot coffee. He handed her one of them before dragging the only chair over to the sofa so he could sit down facing her. "When the children finally left, I had to take a minute to think about what you told me. That Henry Crane is…was…"

As his voice trailed off, Gillian leaned forward, taking his hand gently. "That Henry Crane was your father too," she offered, and he looked back at her, tears running down his tanned cheeks.

"That Henry Crane was…m-my father."

As his voice broke, she cast all her fear away and with a groan dragged him over to the sofa, putting her arms around him. With a whimper he let go of his restraints, and as he cried his pain out, she held his shaking body close to hers, offering him the only thing she could, the quiet love of a sister.

"I'm so sorry," he whispered as the sobbing ended. "I've totally mucked up your pretty blouse."

"No worries," she said with her own crooked grin. "That's what a sister is for. And it's washable," she added.

At first he stared at her, not understanding what she meant, but then a slow smile grew on his face. "That's right. I didn't think of that. If Henry is my father it means you are my sister. My little sister…"

New tears filled his eyes as he put his hand against her cheek, looking at her with so much love she too felt a lump grow.

"Now I get why I always thought you were such a pain in the ass," he joked, and she laughed through her tears, not wanting to think about what she still had to do, the worst thing.

To ask him about Daisy.

Chapter Twelve

To her surprise, he beat her to the subject, with an amused snort.

"Thank God we never became an item," he said with his crooked grin. "That could have been really disastrous, especially as your mother insisted on keeping her mouth shut."

"We didn't?" Gillian whispered hoarsely, and his wonderful grin deepened.

"Of course we didn't. I told you as much the other day, didn't I? And besides, I think you would have remembered if anything *had* happened."

Chuckling over his own joke, he leaned back into the sofa, crossing his long legs in front of him. It was obvious he was starting to accept what she had told him and that he didn't mind the truth. Instead he seemed to embrace the news as if she had given him what he had wanted the most—clarity, and some closure regarding his true parentage. It made her so happy to see his light smile as he absentmindedly stared at his feet, his thoughts miles away.

She didn't want to push on and end his newly found bliss, but she couldn't stop what she had started now. Not when she was so close to finally getting the answer she sought about their senior prom.

"What about the senior prom? Didn't we...you know...*do* something then?"

His smile vanished, and instead he frowned at her, sensing something was bothering her. "Gillian, what's the matter? Why are you asking me about the senior prom? Don't you remember what happened that night?"

She shook her head. "No. I was so drunk from the spiked punch that I haven't a clue what went on after I arrived on Andrew's arm. All I know is waking up in my own bed the morning after, with blood between my legs and feeling very tender. And a couple of weeks later I found out I was pregnant."

This time it was he who stared at her openmouthed. "You don't know who Daisy's father is? Gillian, sweetheart, I'm so sorry. It must have been such an awful experience for you, especially if it was your first time."

"It wasn't so bad, not really. I was a bit sore, that's all. A perfectly normal feeling for someone who had just lost her virginity, I'm told. The worst part was I didn't know who I'd had sex with. I kind of thought it had to be you, considering my feelings for you. But if you say it wasn't…"

"Oh, my God. Did you think I could be Daisy's father? That would have meant… Oh, my God, Gillian!"

"It wasn't you?"

He shook his head with an oddly relieved yet sad smile. "No, it wasn't me. I didn't stay that long. I was over the top angry at everything back then, and when Candy went on an.…uh…errand with another guy, I kind of lost it and left. I went straight home and packed my things and left immediately for the Marine recruiting office."

"Candy, eh?" Gillian teased, too relieved over the

fact he wasn't Daisy's father to stay serious, and he blushed slightly.

"I must admit I have always had quite a big crush on her, but the truth was she never seemed interested in me. She always pushed you in front of her instead, before waltzing away with someone else."

"I'm sorry."

Laughing straight out, he wagged his finger at her. "You better be. It's your fault she and I never got together in the first place. Thank God for that, by the way. As I said the other day, I wasn't ready for a relationship back then and would have destroyed any possible future we might have had, with my insecurity and childish temper."

"I'm sorry," Gillian repeated. "It seems my infatuation with you hurt more people than I could ever have guessed. My mother never liked how I fancied you, and now I know why. You and Candy could have been something if I hadn't been there, playing the part of the Berlin Wall. And not to mention Andrew…"

"I can second that," Luke said with a wry grin. "There you have one young man who wasn't too happy over your warm feelings for me. But then again, he has only himself to blame, because he never said a word to you about it. Oh, everyone else knew, of course. It was kind of hard not to, considering he was always staring at you like a lovesick puppy whenever you were around."

He sat up, staring at her startled face. "Do you think it's possible Matt could be Daisy's father? I know the two of you were dancing rather closely when I left, and I only remember it because I saw Megan standing by the edge of the dance floor watching the two of you, looking more relieved than jealous. I found it quite odd, as she was supposed to be Matt's girlfriend and future wife."

Matthew Barnes.

"No. He couldn't possibly…" Gillian felt the nausea return at full strength. "That would mean Sally Barnes would be Daisy's grandmother."

"A fate worse than death." Luke grinned, and she felt a sudden urge to throw something at him.

"He does have dark hair…"

Luke gave her a curious look. "What does that have to do with Matt being a possible father?"

"Because Daisy's hair is dark, and I come from a family known for being blond."

"That's right," Luke drawled slowly. "Which would mean both Daisy's father and my biological mother are dark-headed."

She nodded solemnly, for now ignoring his input about his mother, focusing on the matter of her heart instead. "Matt is dark-haired."

"He sure is. Which also removes Andy as a possible father, I'm afraid."

She looked up with a smile. "I'm sorry to have to disappoint you, but I know it's not Andy. Besides the fact that he, as you just said, is a very blond man from a very blond family, the truth is we never once were intimate. We were best friends, nothing more."

"He wanted more."

"I know that now, but he never said anything to me about it back then."

"Didn't he take you to the dance?"

"Yes, he did, but he only brought me there. As soon as we arrived he left me in the wind, and I have to admit I forgot about him almost instantly, being on the hunt for you." She giggled as memories from the evening came back to her. "When he picked me up at my mother's house, he showered me with admiration, complimenting me over and over again about how lovely I looked. He had even bought me a corsage with his hard-earned money, and I remember how his hands shook as he put it on my wrist. That moment he was my Prince Charming, making me feel like a real princess. But as soon as we arrived at the prom, he deserted me, and I don't remember seeing him again that evening, not even before the awful punch blurred my memory."

"I remember him, though. I passed him as I was leaving. He was standing behind a pillar at the side of the dance floor, drinking that vile punch you obviously had too much of, and drinking it like a thirsty man drinks water. He never took his eyes off you, watching from the side as you danced with the other boys. When I tried to talk to him, he actually snapped at me, and you know Andrew—he never snaps."

She let out a sad little laugh. "Nothing would have made me happier than if it turned out Andy was the one that night. That he is Daisy's father. But unfortunately I know it wasn't him. He would never have stayed silent afterwards. No, he would have insisted on talking to me about it. But instead he avoided me. The sad truth is we didn't see much of each other that summer. His father was struggling with his bad back, and Andy had to run the whole farm for him. And then my loving mother kicked me out when she found out I was pregnant, and by then it was too late, and I never saw him again. Not until I returned here a couple of weeks ago."

Luke nodded with a disappointed little grimace.

"You are right. Andrew would have said something. Ah, I thought I had it all figured out, and now we are back at square one. Matt."

The mere thought of Matthew Barnes being the father of her beautiful daughter disgusted her. For Daisy's sake, and Megan's, she hoped Luke was wrong.

"I guess I'll just have to ask him, just as I've asked you. It will not be the best moment in my life, that's for sure, having to ask him if he remembers going to bed with me that night." She made a face, and Luke grinned in response.

"He's not as bad as you think. He can't help it that he is the only child of Sally Barnes and so has no option but to follow her lead. It's sad, though, because I think Matt could be something great if he just got out from under his mother's numbing shadow."

"Just the thought of having to admit to Megan that Daisy is her husband's daughter…" Gillian didn't have to finish her sentence. Luke got the drift.

"Gillian, don't fret about it now. Let's just see what happens, one step at time. I'm with you on this, all the way. Not only because I'm your friend but because I'm your brother."

She squinted up at him, snorting lightly. "If you only knew how strange it sounds, hearing you call yourself my brother."

"It does, doesn't it? But I like it. I've never had a sister before, at least not a real sister, and especially not one who already likes me."

"Like you and like you…"

She hooted with laughter as he threw himself on top of her, tickling her wherever he could reach until she gasped breathlessly for mercy.

151

"Do you give up?" he said, pinning her arms down with his hands, and she stuck her tongue out toward him, just as her daughter did when she wanted her mother to know how silly she found her.

"All right, then," he drawled. "Tell me you like me, and I'll let you go."

"No."

"I'll have you pinned down here until you do."

"No."

"Just three small words. I. Like. You."

"No!"

"Oh, for heaven's sake, Gillian. Just tell the idiot you like him so you can come with me. I need to talk with you about something."

Candice stood in the doorway, looking like a mother tired of listening to her two endlessly fighting children. Luke immediately let go of Gillian and scrambled to his feet.

"It's not what you think…"

"Of course it is what I think. I'm not deaf. I heard the whole conversation, every childish word of it. And not just me, I think everyone who happened to be in the church heard the minister order poor Gillian to give up and tell him she likes him."

"I was just making a statement."

It was unstoppable, the laughter bubbling up inside Gillian. Oh, how she had missed this, being with her friends. It had never dawned on her before how lonely she had been for the last thirteen years, because she'd had Daisy to take care of. But now, looking at the grinning Candice and the blushing Luke, she knew she didn't want to be alone anymore.

She needed laughter in her life.

"Do you need help?" Candice held out her hand, and Gillian grabbed it, using it for support as she stood up.

"As a matter of fact, I do. He's just too much for one small woman to handle."

"But not for two…"

Luke never caught the secret smile the two women shared and was completely caught off guard when they threw themselves on him, pinning him down just as he had done to Gillian and tickling him until he cried with laughter.

"Do *you* give up?" Gillian giggled as she let her fingers dig deep into his neck.

"No," he groaned as they intensified their efforts to break him. In the end they had him begging them to end the torture, promising them anything they wanted as long as they just stopped.

"Do you think he will keep his promise?" Candice asked as she and Gillian walked out into Main Street again, leaving a very humbled minister in the vestry to consider his options.

"Of course he will. If not… Let's just say he will think this little session was easy compared to what he will have to endure in the future if he doesn't."

"Oh, I feel so deliciously evil," Candice said with a satisfied smile. "I will savor this for days, maybe even a whole week."

"I wonder what the girls in the front rows at church will think this Sunday when their hero suddenly starts to scowl at them during the sermon instead of his usual flirting. Oh, how I wish it was Sunday already. I can hardly wait!"

They giggled again as they entered the rectory,

very pleased with the outcome of their little dispute with Luke.

"Ah, there you are." Mrs. Cooper came floating out from Luke's kitchen, giving Candice a disapproving glare before ignoring her again for Gillian. "I was just going to leave you a note, but now I don't have to. You just missed Doctor Marshall, Gillian. He was here looking for you. Your mother is getting worse by the minute, and he wanted you to know she doesn't have much time left on this earth, if you want to say goodbye."

"Oh, Gillian!" Candice put an arm around Gillian's shoulders. "I'll go with you if you want. Nobody should have to say goodbye to their mother alone."

Appreciating Candice's immediate and friendly compassion more than she ever could say, Gillian shook her head with a crooked smile of her own. "Thank you, but no. I've already said goodbye to her today. As a matter of fact, I did that just before she once again kicked me out, telling me to never come back. I can't go against her twice, now, can I?"

"Oh, sweetie," Candice whispered, tears in her eyes, earning another harsh look from their old teacher. "She cut you off again? I'm so sorry to hear that. But don't let it get to you. It's her loss, not yours."

"I know. I'm starting to realize that now. But even more importantly, I'm beginning to think returning to Barnesville wasn't so bad after all. So many things that have been bothering me over the years have been revealed since my return. I don't know if it was the knowledge of death closing in or what it was that spooked her, but even my mother opened up and told me things I would never have known otherwise."

"Like?" Candice stared at her curiously, and Gillian could feel Mrs. Cooper's interested presence behind her.

"Like the fact that Luke is my brother."

"What?" Candice gasped. "He is? B-but how…"

"It seems my father didn't hold his marriage vows in too high regard and made a young woman pregnant with a child who later was adopted by the Walkers."

"Oh, my God!" Candice seemed unable to process what Gillian had said. "That's fantastic. And awful, and…and…and…"

"Fantastic?" Gillian laughed, and Candice blushed in response.

"I didn't really mean it like it sounded, but yes, it is fantastic news. I know how much you longed for a sibling when you were young, and now you've got one."

"And that's the only reason you find my news fantastic?"

Candice's blush deepened until her beautiful face was as red as her hair. "I only thought about your wish for a brother or sister, but now that you mention it, it kind of erases loads of walls for my future, yes. Does Luke know?"

"Yes. I had just told him when you found us in the church."

"What did he say?" Mrs. Cooper asked behind her, and Gillian turned to meet the curious eyes of her former teacher.

"I think he was relieved to find out who his real father was. It must be hard for an adopted person to never know where he originally came from and who his biological parents are. At least he now knows who his father was."

Mrs. Cooper frowned, and it was almost as if the wheels in her brain had started to work. "So he still doesn't know who his mother is, then? Did your mother tell you?"

Gillian shook her head. "No. I never asked. I was too upset over the fact that Luke was my blood relative to think about the poor woman who was unfortunate enough to cross paths with my mother."

"Well, it couldn't be too hard to find out who she is, now, could it?" Mrs. Cooper mused. She was obviously going through her mental file cabinet.

"All mother told me was that the young woman continued to live in Barnesville and never married anyone else."

"Oh!" Candice put her hands together in excitement. "What an excellent clue. There's not so many unwed women of our parents' age, are there?"

"Don't." Gillian put a pleading hand on Candice's. "Leave it be. I think it's up to Luke if he wants to pursue this and try to find his birth mother."

Mrs. Cooper nodded, clearly disappointed. "Against my inner wish, I have to agree with you there, Gillian. The mother might not be ready to be found out yet, and who knows, Luke might not want to find her."

"Oh, rest assured"—Gillian laughed—"Luke will definitely go after the poor woman as soon as he's had a chance to think things through. I could see it in his eyes and in the breathless way he mentioned her."

"Poor Luke." Candice sighed, and both Gillian and Mrs. Cooper nodded in silent agreement.

Poor Luke, indeed.

Solemnly they walked into the kitchen and sat

down at the small kitchen table, three completely different women bonded because of the man they all cherished.

"But Gillian…" Candice suddenly frowned. "Am I completely mistaken, or didn't you just say you became upset over finding out that Luke was your brother?"

"I was."

"Why? What's wrong with having Luke as a brother? I thought you liked him."

Biting her lip so she wouldn't laugh, Gillian met the accusing eyes of Candice and Mrs. Cooper, who each loved Luke dearly in her own way. She knew she could keep her reasons away from them and never let them know how irresponsibly she had behaved on senior prom night, but then again, why?

Neither Candice nor Mrs. Cooper was prone to spill gossip. Oh, they received plenty from others, it was a part of their jobs, but mostly they didn't send the information and the rumors they'd heard any further. Which in the end probably was the reason most people so easily opened up to them. They knew their secret would stay there.

But furthermore, and in Gillian's case maybe even more intriguing—both of them had been there the night of the prom. They might have seen or heard something which could shed some light upon Gillian's delicate problem.

"Because I thought there was a possibility Luke could be Daisy's father."

"Oh." Candice's eyes grew wider. "*Oh!*"

"Exactly."

"Dear child. You thought Daisy was the product of a love affair between a brother and a sister? How awful

157

for you."

"Oh, I didn't think so before," Gillian rushed to explain. "I didn't know about this until today, when my mother told me all about it. She, on the other hand, believed this to be the truth ever since Daisy was conceived, and she never said a word about it until now."

"B-but I don't get it," Candice stuttered. "Why would you *think* Luke was the father? I thought you got pregnant after moving to the big city."

"Candice, honey"—Gillian couldn't hold back a loving smile—"why do you think my mother threw me out? I was pregnant, an embarrassment to the Crane family."

"That woman…" Mrs. Cooper's jaw was clenched hard as she stood up and started to move about in the kitchen, as if the feelings inside her were too much for her. "She has destroyed too many lives, and all because of her pride and her prejudice."

Feeling a sudden urge to defend her mother, Gillian went to the old teacher and took the slightly wrinkled hand in hers.

"Don't waste your time hating my mother. In a way, she saved me by sending me away. If I had stayed here, you know Sally Barnes and her hyenas would have done everything they could to destroy me, to make me miserable for becoming pregnant outside matrimony. Instead, I had to grow up pretty fast and find my own way, to be the sole provider for me and my child. We have a good life back home, Daisy and I, a life I now have come to appreciate even more. Returning to Barnesville has made me realize how lucky I am that I got away, considering what a meager life I would have had if I had stayed."

Mrs. Cooper's unreadable gaze never left Gillian's face. "You have Barnesville sounding like hell on earth."

"It *was* hell to me." Rubbing her neck lightly, Gillian sank back against the wall, staring out through the window over the sink. "I know it's not Barnesville's fault I led such an unhappy life here. It's just that, over the years, the pain I felt when I grew up here has made me feel an aversion to the whole community, not just my mother. I'm not happy here, and I thank the Lord every day that when I leave this time it will be for good."

"I can understand your feelings against your mother, because she obviously made you miserable in any way she possibly could, even though I have to admit it probably was unintended. Rachel Crane grew up with a selfish, calculating father who was known to be heartless and cold as ice. He never did anything if he didn't gain something by it. It feels a bit odd standing here defending your mother, but the truth is undeniable—she never stood a chance for happiness."

"She could have left."

"Could she? It was a different world back when she was young, at least here in Barnesville. The only way a woman could survive was to live with her family or to marry."

Gillian snorted angrily. "You make it sound as if she grew up during medieval times and not during the second half of the twentieth century."

"Barnesville *is* different. You've said it yourself—this town is like none other, and so are its citizens."

With another angry snort, Gillian gave an

exaggerated nod. "I couldn't agree with you more. It's like the town got caught in time a hundred years ago and stayed the same even though the rest of the world evolved."

"Why is that so bad?" Not able to stay silent anymore, Candice heatedly joined the discussion. "The world spins faster and faster, and we humans can hardly hold on to life anymore. Here in Barnesville everything is as it always has been, and even though it's not always so fun, at least it's safe and familiar."

What Candice said made sense, but Gillian wasn't ready to listen. Over the years, she had suppressed her feelings so thoroughly that now when her heart's protective walls were crumbling she felt like a volcano, ready to erupt. Anger like none she'd ever known before flooded her veins, and she felt breathless, as if she couldn't get enough air into her lungs.

"Girls, girls," Mrs. Cooper soothed. "Why start a fight over something neither of you are guilty of?"

Somehow she managed to get them back to the kitchen table, and soon they both had large, calming cups of coffee in their hands.

"I'm sorry." Gillian sighed as the last of her unexpected anger left her. "I never meant to lash out at you two like this. It's just that…"

Both Candice and Mrs. Cooper looked at her compassionately as her voice trailed off. They didn't need any more explanation to put themselves in Gillian's shoes.

"Somehow Barnesville brings out the worst in me, and I seem absolutely unable to handle it."

"You could say that again." Candice gave her an impish smile, and Gillian couldn't hold back a giggle.

"Aw, Candice, how much I've missed you."

"And I you."

"I'm sorry I never called."

"I never called either, did I now?" Shrugging lightly, Candice leaned back and put her feet up on the empty chair next to her, ignoring the sour look from Mrs. Cooper. "It's never anyone's fault, you know. To me, it was the normal stuff happening, the days passing by without me noticing how fast time ticked. And to you it must have been too much with everything else. You were only eighteen years old, Gillian. It's amazing you even survived the bus trip! If my mother had thrown me out without anything but the clothes I wore and the baby in my belly, I would have drowned myself in the nearest puddle. But not you. Somehow you succeeded in creating a life, finding a home, getting a job, raising an adorable daughter. All by yourself. No wonder you never thought about the ones you left behind."

Tears pricked her eyes as she listened to Candice's words, and Gillian knew she was about to make a fool of herself again, this time by crying a river in front of her affectionate audience.

"I just don't get how you managed to do it all alone." Sighing deeply, Candice looked ready to burst into tears too. "I mean, you don't even know who Daisy's father is, and still you…manage…"

The table flew back as Candice stood, not noticing the commotion she created with her unusual clumsiness. Too caught up in the revelation that had hit her, she stared wildly at Gillian.

"Candice Lee—" Mrs. Cooper's admonishment was abruptly cut off.

"You *don't* know who Daisy's father is, do you? That's why you *thought* it was Luke. It sounded so strange to me when you said it, but then I was too caught up in the whole brother-versus-sister scenario, I completely missed the core."

Gillian nodded slowly, feeling a bit squeamish as she waited for the reaction.

"B-but how…" Mrs. Cooper stuttered. "How could you not know?"

"You were drunk, weren't you?" Candice face was almost comical as she went from one revelation to another. "It must have been the senior prom, because that is the only time you ever became drunk, and completely without realizing, as you never understood that the punch would be spiked."

"It was," Gillian breathed, and Candice nodded slowly, caught in old memories.

"You came with Andrew, didn't you?" Candice asked, without wanting an answer. "But when you couldn't stop talking about Luke, he got angry and left you, and he spent the evening with loads of beer bottles."

Had she really been that selfish? Humiliated warmth crept over Gillian's cheeks as the answer came back to her, clear as day—yes, she had. She had been so caught up in her own feelings that she had never understood how Andrew felt more for her than friendship.

The more she thought about it, the more embarrassed she became. Suddenly the memory of when he had invited her to the prom came back to her, his urgency when asking her and the radiant joy when she accepted.

He had thought her acceptance of him as her date had meant something more, but she had just thought it a comfortable way to go to the prom. Not once had she thought about Andrew. All she had thought about was Luke.

The boy who never had asked her.

"You danced a lot, but not with Luke," Candice continued slowly, caught in the memories of a party long ago. "I know, because I was depressed enough by watching him quite intensely until he left. But you did dance with Matt for a long time, and it was quite heatedly, if my memory doesn't fail me. I remember I tried to get Megan to interrupt, to fight for her boyfriend, but she didn't want to. All she wanted was to go home. And in the end Matt took her…"

"So it couldn't have been Matthew, then?" Mrs. Cooper mused, caught in the picture Candice's memories painted.

"I don't think so," Candice mumbled thoughtfully. "But then again, all I remember is him taking Megan home. Just because I never saw him again that night doesn't mean he and Gillian didn't meet up later. Everything kind of became a blur to me after Luke left."

Her smile was small and tired, showing without words how pathetic she found herself, and again Gillian felt ashamed at how much she had missed. Not once looking beyond her own infatuation, she had walked all over Andrew's and Candice's feelings, not to mention Luke's. Maybe she had more in common with her mother than she liked to think…

"I'm sorry, Candice…" Gillian began, but Candice silenced her by holding up a finger.

"Don't. It wasn't anyone's fault. We were kids, kids with more emotions than brains."

"But I should have…"

"No, you shouldn't. Neither of us told you about our feelings, did we? We were all too caught up in ourselves to see things differently. I mean, look at me. I was so incredibly in love with Luke, but I never told you, did I? You were my best friend, Gillian. I should have said something but never did. So how could it be your fault?"

"Born to feel guilt, I guess." Gillian grinned and was rewarded with laughter from her audience, which eased the mood in the kitchen.

As if on cue, they changed the subject, instead talking about other things in their joint past which they could laugh over. Lighter subjects that didn't make them feel odd and queasy.

By the time Andrew walked through the door, they had managed to let the sadness go completely, and their laughter filled the air as they busily dissected all the people of Barnesville. As his serious eyes met hers, Gillian's smile faded away and something cold grabbed hold of her heart. When he opened his mouth, she knew what he was about to say, and for a second she wanted to do something, anything, to force him to stay quiet.

But she couldn't. Instead, she grabbed Candice's hand to strengthen herself as Andrew took a hesitant step toward her, the compassion in his beloved face telling her why he had sought her.

"Rachel's dead."

Chapter Thirteen

She cried all over him.

For hours she sat in his lap surrounded by his strong, comforting arms, gradually soaking his favorite shirt with her tears. She hadn't thought she would be this affected by her mother's death, but it only took one tender smile from him and a warm, comforting palm against her cheek for her to break down completely. Sobbing wildly she had stumbled into his waiting arms, hiding her nose in the crook of his neck as he carried her over to the living room and sat down in one of Luke's comfortable armchairs.

Somewhere behind her she'd heard Candice and Mrs. Cooper leave, promising to take care of Daisy for her, but she had been too lost in her grief to find the strength to react to them.

The room was dark when she finally managed to calm herself enough to stop the heartfelt sobs. Still not opening her hurting eyes, she listened to his steady heartbeats against her ear, while his warm breath caressed the top of her head. A glow started to build inside her as his hands slowly worked their way up and down her spine, leaving a path of love wherever they touched.

Why hadn't she realized earlier what a wonderful man he was? Had she been so blinded by what she thought she felt for Luke that she had missed the gem she already had in her hands?

Being too used to having Andrew around, she had never understood how much he really meant to her. Thinking back, she could easily see how he had been the one for her all along. She just hadn't understood what he always had known—they belonged together.

When a contented sigh slipped out of her, she felt his chest rumble as his hearty laughter filled the air, cutting through the sadness and lightening the mood a bit.

"Feeling better, I guess?"

She nodded, careful not to bump his chin as she had the last time she had sought comfort in his arms. "Much better. Thank you."

"Please, honey, don't thank me. There is no other place I would want to be than here, with you in my arms. I just wish…"

His voice trailed off, but she knew what he left unsaid. His life would have been perfect if it hadn't been for her feelings for Luke. With another sigh she straightened herself, feeling his arms almost hesitantly leave her back.

She had so much to tell him, she just needed some space between them so she could think. And light. She definitely needed light so he could recognize the truth in her eyes and the love in her heart.

After turning on the lamp on the sideboard, she moved over to the sofa and sat facing him. He looked tired, his blond hair tousled and dark smudges under his sad eyes. This was not the cheerful, radiant man she had met when returning to Barnesville. No, this man was exhausted, both emotionally and physically, and all because of her.

Not knowing how to begin her confession, she chewed on her lower lip but stopped as she saw his gaze growing hotter as he watched the movement.

"I'm so sorry for everything I've put you through," she started insecurely, and he waved his hand dismissively.

"It's nothing. As I said, to me there is nothing more important than you."

His raw honesty nearly made her all weepy again, but she forced herself to be calm. This was not the moment for more tears.

"Please Andrew, could you just listen to me? There is…something…I need to tell you, and I don't know where to begin."

His eyes never left her face as he leaned back and crossed his arms over his chest.

"Why don't you start from the beginning?" He smiled reassuringly, and she took a deep breath.

"All right. But you have to promise not to interrupt me until I'm finished. There is so much I need to talk to you about, and I want to make sure I tell you everything."

"The whole truth and nothing but the truth?"

She laughed at his joke, and some of the tension inside her started to ease. Why was she so nervous? This was Andrew. *Her* Andrew.

"So help me God," she sighed in response and was awarded another radiant, although tired, smile.

"So…" he prompted, and she took another deep, strengthening breath.

"I love you."

His smile was warm and friendly. "I know, and I love you too."

"No, I mean I *love* you."

"And I you."

She sighed, frustrated. "Andy, you are not listening to me. I *love*-love you."

His smile faltered as the coin finally dropped, and quickly she continued before he had a chance to interrupt her again.

"Ever since I came back to Barnesville, I have been fighting this too-consuming attraction I've felt for you, and every day, every hour—even every minute—it has been harder and harder for me to deny what my heart feels."

He sat up straight, a desperate hope screaming silently from his whole being. "Why deny it? I love you more than I ever can express, a-and if you would...if you love me..."

It was obvious he was searching for the right words to entice her, to make her his, all because she had rejected him too many times over the last couple of weeks and his insecurity made him fear saying something that would make him lose her forever. Instead he held out his hands toward her, reaching for her, and she held up a warning finger.

"You promised me you would let me finish."

"But Gilly..."

"Andrew Marshall!"

He sank back into the chair again. "Yes, yes. Please. Do continue."

"Thank you. What I am trying to say is about the day when I first met you again, outside your office. Do you remember what you said to me when I asked you if you had someone special in your life?"

When he shook his head, she felt like rolling her

eyes. "You told me you did, that you were very much devoted to someone."

"Ah, yes," he said with a relieved smile as the memory of the conversation came back to him. "I meant you, of course. I have always been devoted to you, almost hopelessly so."

Leave it to a man to complicate things.

"Well, I thought you meant you were married to someone else and quite happily so."

"You did?"

"Yes."

"But I'm not married. I've never even been engaged."

"Why not?" She knew it was she who was straying from the subject now, but she couldn't stop herself. She was amazed that such a wonderful man had managed to stay single, and she just had to ask him now when the opportunity presented itself.

He shrugged lightly. "Well, at first I waited for you to come back, but you didn't. And when I learned you had started a new life and a new family of your own I was…hurting…for a long time. I needed time to lick my wounds and find a way to believe in love again. Eventually my mother grew tired of me moping around, I guess, and without caring about what I said she more or less threw me into the arms of different women she considered daughter-in-law material. I must admit I warmed up to a few of them—against my will, mind you—and there was one I even considered proposing to."

"Why didn't you?"

"She wasn't you."

His loyalty was admirable. And incredibly stupid.

"Andy, for heaven's sake! How can you throw your whole life away on a dream you must have been sure could never come true? You knew I had a life somewhere else, so why did you insist on giving up your own chance of happiness and still wait for me?"

"I didn't wait for you."

"You didn't?" This time it was she who didn't understand. "B-but you are not married?"

"I mean I didn't sit around waiting for you. No, I went to New York, searching for you."

Tears filled her eyes. "You did?"

"Yes. And I found you. It wasn't so hard. Not that many Gillian Cranes in the phone book."

"But…"

This time it was he who held up a finger. "Let's just say it wasn't so hard to see you were happy and content with your new life. You had a good home, a good job, and a precious little girl you obviously adored. How could I intrude on that? How could I ask you to leave your perfect life and come back home with me?"

"Why didn't you come up to me, talk to me?"

He sighed and laughed at the same time. "Because I didn't want to meet the man in your life. I was still hurting badly over you leaving me, and I knew I would never be able to stand seeing you gaze at another man with love. So I went back home again, told my father I didn't want to be a farmer, and went to medical school instead. I became a doctor, took over the Barnesville practice, and then one day when I walked out the front door I met you, looking up at me with your lovely eyes, and fell just as helplessly in love with you all over again."

"And continued with telling me you were married."

"I never said that," he scoffed.

"Maybe, but that was what I thought you said."

"You could have asked."

"Yes, you are right—I could have. In fact, I tried but got interrupted every time. And then, too, you and everyone else kept talking about your Wife, the very cuddly one you had at home."

"That's my cat." He snorted. "Everyone knows that."

"I didn't."

"You thought…"

She nodded. "Yes, I did."

"But…"

"It never occurred to you I hadn't heard about how you got a cat you named Wife? I hadn't been in town for thirteen years. How could I have known?"

"I didn't think—"

"No, you didn't," she interrupted rudely, her voice shivering with emotion. "No one did. Do you know how badly I've felt about lusting after another woman's husband? God, I've been feeling so sick over how you again and again showed me how much you wanted me, how much you loved me. And all the time I thought we both knew there was another woman waiting for you at home."

He didn't say a word. Speechless, he stared at her, trying to grasp the full meaning of what she told him. Angrily she wiped her tear-filled eyes with the back of her hand. Now she knew he was innocent, but the remembrance of how she had felt when she thought she was in love with a married man who wanted her still disturbed her. For her it had been real.

171

"Your behavior even had me trying to seduce poor Luke," she snarled, and that woke him from his stupor.

"I definitely did not throw you in Luke's direction. If I remember correctly, it was *you* who asked *me* to take you to him. Do you know how much *that* hurt?"

She could imagine. The heat went out of her as she saw his confusion which now was mixed with a silent, desperate hope.

"About Luke," she started over and had his immediate attention. This was obviously a subject he was very interested in, her feelings for his friend. "I was so fascinated by him as a teenager, and not only because of his good looks and very attractive James Dean air, like all the other girls. What allured me the most was his rebellious independence and his indifference to everyone else and what was said about him. There I was, an open wound, hurting under my mother's unfeeling thumb, desperate for just an ounce of his self-confidence. There was nothing more I wanted than to be like him, and therefore he became everything I wanted."

"So you didn't love him then?"

"Oh, yes, I did. With all the romantic foolishness a teenage girl can muster. He was my Prince Charming, and I would have died for him if he had asked me to. But it was a shallow love, Andy, and I know that now. Back then… Let's just say I thought it was enough for me, because I was just a child."

She reached over the small table and grabbed his large, warm hands. "What I didn't understand then was how my feelings for you were so much more. You were my best friend, and I trusted you completely. You made me feel whole and at ease, and when I was with you I never felt alone or afraid because you lifted me."

"Lord, you make me sound so boring." His laughter warmed her heart, and she strengthened her grasp of his hands.

"What I felt for Luke was a young girl's romanticized vision of love, but my feelings for you were a woman's. I was just too young to recognize the latter was the real thing. The true love."

"Come here," he growled, pulling her hands lightly toward him.

She shook her head with a small smile.

"No."

"Honey, your words are making me too happy. I need you here so I can touch you."

"I'm still not finished, and if you don't stop interrupting me like this I will never be."

He sighed deeply. "All right. Keep going, but do hurry up, please. I'm desperate to kiss you."

With all the love she felt she looked back at him. "Me too."

She felt his hands tremble, but he never said a word. Instead he let go of her and sat back, again crossing his arms over his chest, silently prompting her to continue. She knew what his game was: the sooner she spat out what was in her heart, the sooner he could kiss her and touch her as much as he wanted. She hadn't thought she was able to love him more than she already did. But now she knew she could.

Wanting nothing more than to be near him, she jumped to the next part, unmerciful. "Luke's my brother."

"What?"

"He is. This morning, when my mother more or

less told me to leave her and never come back, she also spilled a few secrets of her own, one being that Luke is my father's illegitimate child."

"Oh."

"Stop looking so damned pleased." She laughed, and his grin deepened.

"Do continue, honey. I'm even more desperate to touch you now, when I know you'll never fall for Luke's rebellious handsomeness again."

"Andy…"

"Does Luke know?"

"Yes. That's why I had to go to him this morning, because I wanted to tell him what my mother had said."

Losing his grin, Andrew frowned at her. "Why didn't you tell me? I thought you once again were discarding me for him. All you did was ramble on about going to Luke's, when I tried to help you."

"I had to tell him first."

"No, you didn't. You could have told me, and then I could have gone with you, supporting you."

"I had to go by myself, Andy. There's more to the story, and I-I wasn't ready to face you with that just yet. I still am not, but I know I'll have to confess my sins to you sooner or later. But for now that specific sin will have to wait. There is so much more I want to tell you, and…"

"Gillian, stop it. You don't have to excuse yourself to me. Whatever it is, we can deal with it later, together, when you are ready. Just skip that part and move on."

"All you care about is kissing me." She snorted, and he grinned more as he wiggled his eyebrows at her.

"Guilty as charged."

She should be upset with him for dismissing her

secrets so easily, but then again, his obvious need to be with her made her warm all over.

"Aren't you curious at all?"

"Of course I am, but now that I know we have all the time in the world, I can wait until later, preferably with my lips plastered on yours."

"Not all the time in the world," she admitted and he lost his grin again, sensing her seriousness.

"Why not?"

"Because I'm leaving Barnesville soon. I'll stay until mother's…funeral…but as soon as I've settled her affairs, Daisy and I are going back home. Back to our lives."

"Can't you two move here?"

She shook her head. "No."

Silently he stared at her, his blue eyes unreadable, for such a long time she was practically squirming when he finally opened his mouth. "Then I'm coming with you."

She hadn't expected that. Not so quickly, at least. They hadn't even talked about their relationship yet, and what they wanted out of it, and yet he was ready to follow her to the end of the world. Or to her home in New York.

"You don't have to do that. You have a good life here. Think about your job. Your family. Alma would never forgive me if you leave."

"Of course she will. She's my mother. All she wants is to see me happy, and I know now the only way I can be happy is to be with you. And if it means I have to leave Barnesville… So be it. I've waited for you all my life. How can I let you go now, when you finally are mine?"

She couldn't wait any longer. With a sob she jumped over the small table, landing with a thud on his lap.

"Oof," he groaned, but she didn't apologize. Instead, she did what they both wanted so badly—she kissed him.

Again he groaned, but this time out of passion. Deepening the kiss, she ran her fingers through his hair to hold his head steady while she ravished his mouth. His hands pressed her body hard against his, as if he was afraid she would leave if he let her move away from him in the slightest.

She didn't know how long they sat there, but when they finally broke apart it felt like eons of time had passed. She let her hands caress his muscular arms, rejoicing in knowing he was hers to touch as much as she wanted to.

"You are mine," he whispered hoarsely, and she nodded, tears in her eyes once more.

"Always."

"Don't ever leave me again."

"I won't."

"Because if you do I'll hunt you down and drag you back, just so you know."

"You better." She laughed. "If you don't, I promise you I'll hunt you down to tell you just what I think about you not hunting me."

He drew her closer again, and she settled with her head under his chin and his arms surrounding her. Without words he made her feel more loved than she had ever been in her whole life, and for some strange reason she felt sorry for her mother, who had never had the opportunity to know the strength love gave.

Rachel Crane might have had a horrible childhood, but it shouldn't have stopped her from loving her own child. But then again, Gillian decided as she thought about it, maybe she had, in her own way, just as Mrs. Cooper said.

Maybe it was Gillian who was the one who should have seen what she'd had with *her* mother, instead of constantly watching what everyone else had and always wishing for more, just as she had with Andrew. Alma too had mentioned to her she thought Rachel didn't know how to show Gillian what was in her heart, too used to pushing her own daughter away.

And now it was too late.

Rachel was dead, and Gillian would never know if her mother had loved her. And she would never be able to show her mother how much she meant to her. The truth was that Gillian had loved her mother with all her heart, no matter what she tried to convince herself of, and she had spent too many nights crying her heart out until she fell asleep from exhaustion.

"Thinking about Rachel?" Andrew's voice was low and compassionate, effectively calming her down because of the love he wrapped around her like a snuggly blanket.

"Yes. I wish she'd known how much I loved her."

"Oh, I promise you, she did know. And furthermore, she loved you with all her heart."

She sat up again, frowning as she saw his sober honesty. "Did she tell you that?"

"No. Not straight out, but I knew anyway. You see, when I became her doctor, I had quite a hard time getting close to her, something which was quite frustrating, considering her bad heart and need of care.

But after a while I noticed there was one thing which made her calm down and let me come closer, and that was when we talked about you. In the end, all we did was talk about you. Or I talked and she asked. It was as if she wanted to relive your childhood by listening to what we had done."

His words were like manna on her soul, and she hung on his every word, desperate to hear anything about her mother's feelings for her person.

"You know, when I first told her you were back in town she became almost hysterically happy, ordering me around to fetch a certain dress and help her with her hair. But then her friends came and started to spread their venom, and it was saddening to see how your mother lost her breathless expectation and became almost irritated over your return."

"Sally Barnes."

He nodded slowly. "She is pure evil, that woman. If you only knew what Matt has told me about her…"

He sighed heavily but didn't finish, and she stayed quiet, sensing this was not the time or place to pursue the subject. Instead she put her arms around his neck, giving him another lingering kiss, which effectively removed the sad thoughts of her mother for the lighter thoughts of her future with this wonderful man.

She didn't want to think about Sally Barnes and her followers, who turned Barnesville into hell on earth with their small-minded evilness. All she wanted was to think about her future, which in a few stormy hours had moved her from loneliness to having both a man and a brother in her life.

And friends.

Both Candice and Megan had made sure what they

once had still remained. Their friendship hadn't disappeared over the years. Instead, it seemed to have grown stronger even though Gillian had been absent.

Not to mention Alma and Mrs. Cooper, two formidable ladies in their own right, who with their mature wisdom had helped her sort her confused thoughts so she could think clearly.

It was a scary thought that she had more people who cared about her here in Barnesville than she had in New York, where she had spent the last thirteen years of her life. She had been too busy with her work and taking care of Daisy to ever feel the need to respond to any of the few offers of friendship she had received.

But now she had Andrew…

Again tears filled her eyes. Unable to resist the emotions storming inside her, she hugged him closer, unable to grasp that he was all hers. Never again would she be lonely. Never again would she feel alone and on the outside.

Now they were two, together.

No, she thought with a wry smile as she heard the front door slam shut and her daughter's light voice calling her, now they were three.

"Mom, why are you sitting in Andrew's lap?" Daisy asked as she walked into the dim living room, without mercy turning up the lights until it was bright enough to think the sun had joined them.

"Because she loves me," Andrew said matter-of-factly, squinting in what he thought was Daisy's direction, and she rewarded him with a very telling roll of her eyes.

"Yuck!" She grimaced, and Gillian bit back a smile. Leave it to an almost-teenager to remove the magic of the moment.

"I guess I'll have to get used to this," Andrew mumbled into her ear, and she nodded, trying hard to stay serious as he sighed heavily, his broad shoulders slumping. "Life will never be the same again with the three of us under the same roof. I can feel it."

"What? Are we moving in with you?"

The radiant joy in Daisy's face told Gillian she didn't have to fear her daughter's reaction to the news of Andrew becoming her stepfather. The girl obviously already adored him, and a look at his just-as-happy face when he gave her a reassuring nod told her just how much he liked Daisy.

"Actually, he's coming with us."

"To New York?"

"Yes."

"Oh."

Frowning, Gillian left Andrew's lap and went to her daughter. "You don't sound happy about going home. I thought you longed for all your friends."

"I do. Really, I do. But... It's just that my friends here are so much more fun. We *do* things, not just sit around talking about boys and clothes and other boring stuff."

"You can play with them whenever we're here, visiting Andy's family."

"That's not the same," Daisy whined. "I don't want to go back to New York. I'm not allowed to do anything there. You are so much more afraid of everything back home, and here in Barnesville you aren't. Here you let me run around as much as I want to, wherever I want to."

"But Daisy..."

Growling with frustration, Daisy threw her arms into the air before turning and barging out through the door to disappear into the darkness. Calling out her name, Gillian followed her distressed daughter, but by the time she got outside the rectory, Daisy was nowhere to be seen.

Anger, mixed with fear and frustration, filled her as she stared out into the shadows of the night, hoping to see the silhouette of her stubborn. runaway daughter, but in vain. Daisy was probably hiding somewhere, making sure her mother wouldn't find her.

Andrew's arms circled her waist, and with a sigh she leaned back against his body as he placed a chaste kiss on her temple.

"Do you think she's okay?"

"Yes, she's okay. She's just a bit angry, that's all."

"A bit?" He chuckled. "I wouldn't call what your lovely daughter just unleashed *a bit* angry."

"In Daisy's world it was a bit."

"You mean she gets worse?"

Gillian laughed and patted his hands, which rested against her belly. "There is no end to the feelings of a teenager, and she's getting them early."

"God have mercy," he said, sounding quite overwhelmed, and she laughed again.

Just as she was about to close the door, Daisy snuck in, looking both headstrong and embarrassed. Her daughter knew she had misbehaved but obviously felt too strongly about the subject to give her mother the apology she deserved. Instead she walked past them without meeting their eyes, and disappeared into her bedroom.

Andy winced as Daisy closed her bedroom door

with a bang.

"Maybe moving in with us isn't as good an idea as you first thought." Gillian laughed, and Andy smiled back.

"Now that you mention it…"

She turned around, still in his embrace, and put her arms around his neck. "Ah, Andy. If you only knew how much I look forward to our future. It's so strange. I don't have any fears about it at all, which is so unlike me. I usually fear everything."

He put a lingering kiss on the tip of her nose, and she closed her eyes, savoring the sweet sensations; her whole body tingled. The next kiss wasn't as subtle, as his lips finally found hers.

It was like no other kiss.

The trembling love, the shivering happiness, and the quivering hope of the future made it perfect. As his hands travelled down her body, creating waves of heat as they went, she knew this was it.

This was *her* man.

"I want you so badly," Andrew moaned against her neck, and she closed her eyes in pure pleasure as his breath washed over her shivering skin.

"Come." Tugging his hand brazenly, she moved backwards toward the door that led to the rest of the boarding house.

"Are you sure?" His voice was hoarse, strained with an evident, overwhelming need to be with her.

When she nodded lightly, he looked almost as if he were in pain as he followed her out into the hallway and into her bedroom. She finally had him to herself, inside her bedroom and in her life, and she didn't waste any time.

Neither did he.

She hardly had time to kick the door shut behind her before she had him all over her. His large hands pressed her closer to him after removing every last thread of her clothing, and his hot mouth explored in pulsating paths over her body as each area was displayed to his roaming eyes.

Moaning, she pulled his clothes off too, not satisfied until she could feel the soft hair on his torso against her hands, against her bare breasts. Tenderly he put his arms around her, lifting her and carrying her to the bed.

Dizzy with need to have him closer, to have him deep inside her, she stretched her arms around him, forcing his mouth closer to hers.

"Ah, woman, you drive me crazy." He laughed into her mouth. "If you don't slow down, I'm not gonna be able to hold back, and this will come to one embarrassing stop."

"I don't mind," she purred, too aroused to care about foreplay or slowly building the fire. "All I want is you. Now."

He groaned as he gave in to her—not too unwillingly, she noticed. As she felt him slide deep inside her, her body wanted to explode from joy and earthmoving passion.

The lovemaking was more satisfying than she ever could have fantasized. It was like their bodies were made for each other. The fit was perfect, and as he came deep into her she too found a fulfillment which left her a panting, sweaty pile of happiness.

"Thank you," she whispered as he rolled off her, lying on his side and watching her with more love than she had ever before seen.

"You're welcome." His smile was slow and satisfied. "And please feel free to use me again, whenever you feel the need to."

They laughed softly together over the silly joke, and she felt tears fill her eyes as she looked at the gorgeous man that now was hers. All she could see, from the too-long blond hair down to those too-hairy toes, was hers.

She just had to kiss him again. And again. Soft vulnerable kisses that made her quiver with delight. Not until Andy's phone rang, taking them back to reality, did their lips part.

"I have to go," Andrew announced, sighing, when he turned the cell phone off. "A patient of mine is getting worse."

"Go," she urged, feeling oddly supportive about his sudden departure as they each dressed rapidly. She, who always had hated when she was deserted, found it almost liberating he had to go. That he had somewhere he was needed.

"I can come back later," he said as he headed for the small gate out of the yard, his head already filled with what needed to be done.

"No need," she assured him. "Why don't we meet at the diner for lunch tomorrow instead? Say noonish?"

"Noon it is," he called out over his shoulder as he jumped into his old truck, sending her all the love he felt with one last look.

She lifted her hand in greeting as he drove away, watching the red taillights until they disappeared at the Main Street bend. She felt exhausted. It had been a long day, with so much emotional turbulence she almost staggered as she walked back into the rectory.

As Gillian headed toward Daisy's bedroom, she knew she should talk to her daughter about what had happened and what feelings lay behind such a burst of anger. But she was too tired. Instead she silently made sure her daughter brushed her teeth before tucking into bed.

There were more important things for her to talk to Daisy about, things she hadn't had a chance to tell yet, as her daughter had been out roaming the neighborhood all day.

"My mother passed away today," Gillian said softly, knowing it was best to spit the truth out, when it came to Daisy. Her daughter had never liked when she tried to ease the truth for her.

"Oh, Mom," Daisy cried with compassion, throwing her arms around Gillian's neck. "I'm so sorry. You must be so sad."

"I am," Gillian admitted, and to her surprise her eyes filled with tears as her daughter's simple and spontaneous reaction brought it all back to her.

"Were you there with her when she died?"

"No. I wasn't."

Daisy leaned her head to the side, watching her mother's face with her honest blue eyes. "I'm glad you weren't. I think it's better you remember the good parts instead."

"I must admit I'm kind of glad myself I wasn't there when she passed away. Mother wasn't herself these last weeks, so angry and rude. She wasn't like that when I was young; she never misbehaved. Always calm and always there. I must admit I would rather remember the good parts, just as you said. I want to savor the good memories."

Daisy nodded, her sweet face seeming oddly mature even with her girly nightgown and pigtails. "Never forget."

Pressing her palm against her daughter's smooth cheek, Gillian gave her a tear-filled smile as she repeated the two words. "Never forget."

"I love you, Mommy," Daisy whispered, leaning closer to Gillian and hugging her closely. "Promise me you'll never die."

"I can't promise you that," Gillian said, tenderly stroking her daughter's dark hair. "But I do promise you I will never stop loving you and I'll always be there for you, no matter what."

A hiccup was all she got for an answer, and she placed a sweet kiss on the top of Daisy's head. It wasn't easy to understand everything in life when you were a mere twelve years old. Her daughter mostly did a good job with trying to understand, but sometimes even she lost her insight.

"Do we have to go back?"

"Yes."

"All right." The sigh was deep and dejected. "Is Andrew really coming with us?"

"Yes, he is."

"That's nice."

Gillian continued stroking Daisy's hair slowly, afraid any sudden change in pace would break the moment of closeness. "You think so?"

"Uh-hum. I like him. He's funny."

"He likes you, too."

"Of course he does. He has to."

Shaking her head slightly, Gillian couldn't help

feeling proud of her unbending, self-assured daughter. There wasn't much in this world that made Daisy break. She knew what she wanted, and she believed in other people. Two things which made her more or less unstoppable.

Of course Andrew had to like her. Daisy was simply too adorable to resist. He would make an excellent stepfather for her daughter, showing her the way of a good man. Daisy had always acted a bit strangely toward men, especially the few men Gillian had dated. It was as if she always was searching for her father and couldn't accept anyone else. As though she were almost desperate.

Just as she was when they first arrived in Barnesville. Then, Daisy had determinedly turned every rock she could find and had engaged every last child in town, searching for a dark-haired man who missed a daughter.

But as Gillian thought about it, she realized Daisy hadn't talked much about finding her father during the last couple of days. As a matter of fact, she hadn't mentioned it much at all, which was odd, considering how fanatic she had been when they first arrived.

"Is it because of your father you don't want to leave Barnesville?" she asked, trying to not sound too interested in hearing the reply.

"No." Daisy left her mother's embrace, leaning back so Gillian could look into her sweet face. "Of course it isn't. He won't be here anyway."

"He won't?" Gillian frowned and was rewarded with another hefty roll of her daughter's eyes.

"Of course he won't. You just said it yourself: he's coming with us to New York."

Chapter Fourteen

Holding the hot cup of coffee between her hands, Gillian let the rising heat warm her tired face as her thoughts wandered back to last night. After announcing that Andrew was her father, Daisy had promptly turned over and fallen asleep, leaving Gillian filled with doubt and confusion.

How could Daisy be so certain Andrew was the one? The girl never was this matter of fact about anything if she wasn't completely sure she was right. But how could she know? It wasn't as if she had been there...

While her daughter had slept like a baby the whole night through, Gillian had tossed and turned, unable to stop herself from going over and over again the few memories she had from the senior prom. Reliving every moment, she couldn't find anything different from before, nothing to show Andrew was the one.

Now, when she knew for certain Luke wasn't either, it was more likely it was Matthew Barnes who had sired Daisy. Just the mere thought of him being the father of her child made her shiver. What if the adorable Daisy was carrying the cold, hateful genes of Sally Barnes? Another shiver ran down her spine, and in that moment Gillian knew Matthew wasn't the father.

It didn't matter what she remembered, she knew in

her heart it wouldn't have mattered how drunk she was, she would never, ever have had sex with him. She had never liked his sneaky ways, and to get her into bed he would have used ever last trick he had.

She would more likely have thrown up all over him than have let him anywhere near her.

Andrew, on the other hand, she wouldn't have refused anything. She trusted him completely, always had, and would have walked over burning coals if he'd asked her to. Luke, Candice, and Mrs. Cooper all had told her he had become drunk out of jealousy and kept watching her from the shadows the whole night.

He must have seen Luke leaving and, knowing how pathetic she had been when it came to the man of her dreams, she figured she would probably have been devastated. You didn't have to be Einstein to figure out that Andrew, with his soft heart and burning love for her, couldn't stand seeing her alone and miserable.

He would have at least asked if there was anything he could do for her, no matter how drunk he was. His concern would have turned her all mushy, because with him she never pretended to be something she wasn't. She'd always liked his lap in her sad moments.

Combine a lovesick, drunk teenage boy and a heartbroken, drunk teenage girl who loved and trusted each other… The outcome could only have been one.

Daisy.

Why had she never thought about this before? It wasn't as if she hadn't been pondering who Daisy's father was, over and over again, during the last thirteen years. But then again, she hadn't known about Luke's departure before. She had always thought he had been there all night and kept nursing a silly hope of him being the one.

To be completely honest, she had more or less believed Luke was the father and had dissected what he had said and done repeatedly. She had never really considered anyone else and therefore never thought twice about what they said and their actions.

Especially not Andrew's.

She remembered his radiant face when he came to get her, his proud admiration of her loveliness in her prom dress. He had made her feel so special, so pretty, and when he put the corsage around her wrist she had felt like she was a princess.

But in the end all his efforts hadn't mattered—as soon as they'd arrived at the dance she had most rudely started to chase after Luke, leaving Andrew and his secret hopes crushed.

She remembered talking to him the next day, but she had suffered the worst kind of hangover and had been in shock at what had happened to her without her remembering with whom. But now, when she thought of it, he had been unusually expectant, as if there was something on his mind but he wanted her to bring it up first.

But she never had.

And then Tom Marshall had hurt his back, so that Andrew had to work day and night at the farm. They had never had the chance to talk again before her mother sent her away. It shouldn't have been so hard for him to figure out she had no memory of what had happened. She knew she had said over and over again that she would never drink so much again, moaning over and over how sick she was.

He hadn't pushed, but then again, he thought he

had all the time in the world to talk with her. Neither of them had known then she soon would leave Barnesville, leave him, and be gone for thirteen years.

"Do you want more coffee?"

The large basket with newly dried laundry landed on the kitchen table with a loud thud, spreading the wonderful scent of sundried cloth. Alma stretched her back slightly, groaning as she joined Gillian at the old, worn kitchen table.

"No, thanks. I'm sorry to disturb you like this. It's just that I have to talk to Andrew…"

"Oh, stop it. You don't have to apologize about being here. This is your home too, always has been and—if I have interpreted my son's radiant smile correctly—will be so even more in the future."

A telling blush crept over Gillian's cheeks, and Alma's smile was just as radiant as Andrew's.

"I knew it! He didn't say a word about it when he arrived last night, but I just knew it. Oh, Gilly, I'm so happy!"

The hug was filled with love and unmistakable welcome, and Gillian closed her eyes, enjoying the motherly show of affection. If Alma became this happy over Gillian finally becoming a part of their family, she knew the older woman would probably explode with joy when she learned Daisy was her biological granddaughter.

But first Gillian had to talk to Andrew. Before they continued on their life together, they desperately needed to have the conversation they should have had thirteen years ago, the morning after the prom.

"They should be back any minute now. Andrew was just helping Tom with the fence over at the old

191

mill. They have been struggling with it for months now, ever since that blasted storm last winter knocked most of it over."

"He has?" Gillian swallowed the panic which started to rise inside of her. "I-I thought you had men employed to deal with stuff like that."

"No, not any more. Since the economy started to fall, it's been too expensive for us to have men around for the upkeep of the farm as we used to do. We have to manage with the hands we've got, and we are lucky to have Andrew and the girls. He's the only one who has moved out from here—the girls are still living with us, and we all struggle to keep the farm afloat."

"Have you ever considered selling it?"

"Of course we have. Tom even had a real estate agent here, trying to get a price for the place. But the kids became furious with us for even thinking about selling it. We didn't know, Tom and I, how much it meant to them, and to be completely frank—I don't think they knew it either, not until they risked losing it."

"Thank God for the children," Gillian mumbled, and Alma nodded in agreement, wiping the corner of her eye with her apron.

"We know we are lucky. Without those three, we would never have been able to stay put. This farm has been in the Marshall family for centuries, and I think it would have been the death of Tom if he had lost it." She laughed through the tears. "No matter what he says, he still needs this place. You know, he actually talked about us going on cruises instead, for the money we would get for the farm. Cruises..."

Alma laughed over her husband's silliness, not noticing how Gillian felt smaller and smaller with every word said.

How could she ever allow Andrew to move with her to the city? It didn't matter that he had said it himself yesterday. She could never force him to leave the Marshall farm or the life he had here. He would never say it, but she knew in her heart he must have already regretted his rash decision to follow her.

So what options were left for them? A long-distance relationship, which would soon have their need to be together faltering and dying? Both of them had too many responsibilities to others in their lives, responsibilities neither of them could escape.

Love wasn't the problem; finding the time for each other was.

How could a doctor at the beck and call of everyone, and with a farm to take care of besides, find time to leave Barnesville even for a day? And how could she, who had Daisy to take care of when she wasn't at her time-consuming job, ever be able to sneak away to meet up with him somewhere?

For her to move halfway, and by doing so cut down the hours it took for them to drive to each other, seemed pointless. They would still have the same problems. And to drag Daisy away to some other town where she knew no one and had no connections at all would be downright cruel.

Another option was breaking up with Andrew immediately, before they even started out. It was probably the sanest option of them all, but she knew in her heart she couldn't live without him anymore. She needed him in her life, because to her he *was* life.

And furthermore, breaking up with him now meant complicating things for him with Daisy, and that was something she never could do to him, or to her daughter. She could of course keep the secret to herself, never let him know about the daughter they shared. But that thought was so far from her wishes she let go of it immediately.

So what was left?

Nausea washed over her as she realized the only reasonable option was for her to move to Barnesville. To leave her home in New York and willingly, literally, go to hell. Daisy wouldn't mind; her tantrum yesterday had told Gillian as much.

As Alma started to make lunch, Gillian numbly folded the laundry, desperately in need of something to do so her thoughts wouldn't drive her crazy. Just as she neatly put down the last pair of trousers on the table, the door slammed, announcing the arrival of Andrew and his father.

"Gillian."

Andrew's face was a study of love as he saw her standing there in his parents' kitchen. Without caring about their audience, which was more than a little interested, he hauled Gillian into his arms. His mouth immediately found hers, and with a contented sigh she kissed him back, too engrossed in the magic that was him to care about being watched.

"There, there." Alma chuckled. "I'm serving lunch in a minute, so stop trying to eat poor Gillian up."

Slowly Andrew lifted his head, breaking the endearing kiss. Gillian was grateful he held her, because she felt so dizzy with the emotions he created inside her she knew she would have fallen quite embarrassingly to the floor if he'd let go.

"Good morning, my love," he mumbled softly,

placing a tranquil kiss on the tip of her nose.

"Good morning, my everything," she whispered in response and was rewarded with one of his radiant smiles, the one that had his blue eyes sparkling.

"How are you doing on a morning like this?"

"Absolutely fabulous."

"Really?"

"Really."

"Any change of heart?"

She shook her head, and he sighed, relieved.

"Thank God. I was a little unsure, thought it might have been just one of my normal daydreams."

"Don't be too happy just yet, son," Tom Marshall called out from the other side of the kitchen. "You have never shared a home with a woman before, but you'll soon become aware it's a life filled with landmines."

"Thomas Marshall," Alma reprimanded her husband sharply, but Gillian could see the lovely lady's eyes dancing with mirth. "Have you forgotten me and his sisters? Aren't we women?"

"Not to him you aren't. No, I meant a woman he cares what he looks like for. As soon as Gillian sees his morning face, whiskers and all, she'll be running as fast as she can from here and back to New York."

Andrew's smile faltered slightly at the mention of the city, and she knew what he thought of—his promise to go with her. Before he had a chance to say something about it to his parents, she nudged his arm, catching his attention again.

"Come," she said lightly. "Why don't you and I leave your parents with the cooking and have a little talk in the other room?"

"Oh-oh!" Tom Marshall boomed, and she could

see a small frown marring Andrew's forehead as he silently followed her through the door into the living room, closing it tightly behind them.

"What's up?" Andrew asked, and she could see he was starting to get anxious.

"Did you fix the fence?" she asked instead of answering his question, and he nodded solemnly.

"Almost. There's one part left which we will have to take care of another day. Father's back gets tired so quickly nowadays."

"Who will help him if you're not around?"

"No one. He'll have to manage by himself."

"Can he?"

Andrew's frown deepened. "Probably not. Gillian, what is this? Why are you asking me all these questions? Are you trying to get me to change my mind about us? Because I promise you I won't. I have waited for you my whole life. There is no way I'm letting you go now when you finally are mine."

Unable to stand there any longer not touching him, she forced him to sit down, placing herself in his lap, just as they had been sitting quite a lot lately. Immediately his large, warm hands found their way around her waist, hugging her closer to him.

"I love you, Andrew Marshall, and all I want to do is to spend the rest of my life with you."

He didn't bother to hide the tears filling his eyes, and he looked like a giddy little boy as he laughed happily. "I'm so glad to hear that, because it's my wish too."

"So I guess we have agreed about wanting to spend the rest of our lives together?"

He chuckled softly. "Yes, we have."

"But where?"

He gave her an amused look. "In New York. That's what we said yesterday."

"What if I feel I can't take you away from here, away from your life, your job, and your parents?"

"Then lose the feeling. Gilly. I knew exactly what I was saying when I agreed to move to you and Daisy in New York. There always a need for good doctors everywhere, and as I happen to be an excellent one, I will have no problem getting a job closer to your home."

"Your humbleness amazes me."

He grinned again. "It does, doesn't it? Jokes aside, I've already had plenty of job offers from the largest hospitals in most of the larger cities on the east coast, so really—there is no need for you to fret about this."

Why was she surprised? She knew what a good man he was and how he excelled in his line of work. Of course there were hospitals that had heard about him and wanted him to join their staff.

"But what about your life here? How do you think your parents will cope when you're not around to help them with the farm?"

He sighed deeply. "That's something which made my decision much harder. I know they need help, but it doesn't mean it has to be me. Any job in the city will pay me more than what I earn today, and I was thinking maybe we could spare some money and pay a hired hand for them. It would mean they could keep the farm and not have to do everything themselves."

He really had thought of everything, and for some reason it annoyed her that he had. It felt as if the package which was their new life together was already wrapped up neatly, ribbon and all. And strangely enough, for being a person who hated spontaneity and surprises, she wanted their life together to be an open book. She wanted them to fill the blank pages on a day-to-day basis, not just follow a premade plan.

"Today you see your parents every day. If you move to the city, you'll probably see them only twice every year, maybe on the summer holiday and at Christmas. And that is in good years."

"Silly Gilly House Mouse, are you sure you're not trying to make me change my mind about us? Because from my point of view it feels like you are desperately searching for reasons to have me stay put."

"Maybe I am."

"Why? I thought you just agreed to us wanting to spend the rest of our lives together?"

"I still do."

"So why all these questions to make me hesitate about leaving Barnesville?"

She put her hands against his cheeks, forcing him to look directly at her so he wouldn't miss that she told the truth. "Because I think it is Daisy and I who should move here, not the other way around."

He stared at her, speechless, and she quickly grabbed the moment, continuing before he had a chance to find a word.

"You know how much I hate the life I had here in Barnesville, and how I would rather live anywhere else in the world but here. But I have come to the conclusion that I might have changed my mind a little lately. I'm not the same person I was back then. I'm someone else today. And to be completely honest, coming back here doesn't mean I'm putting on the same old shoes, carrying on the same old life. I might not love the town, and I certainly don't love all its citizens. But I do love you so much, and if your happiness and Daisy's relies on us living here, then so be it. Let's move here."

"So you will give up everything you have in New York to come and live here, in a town you hate? I don't think you understand what it is you are saying."

"Oh, no? So when I say that all I have back home is a job with a decent income and a daughter who would rather live here, it still sounds unbelievable to you? I have no friends there. I have never had time to make any."

"But your job…"

"Job-schmob," she spat out, surprising herself with her sudden uncaring attitude. Andrew's eyes suddenly sparkled with mirth, and she too had a hard time keeping her serious face. "It's a good job, well paid, but to be honest not a very interesting one. I don't need the money, not here in Barnesville anyway. I'll just sell Mother's awful house and invest the money in your parents' farm instead. Then they can still get the help they need and I will have you home for dinner almost every day."

His smile was slow but honest. "Are you sure?"

"I am."

"You'll hate it here."

"I'll love living with you more."

"There aren't many jobs here."

"I know. I'll think of something."

"You make it sound so easy."

"Wouldn't it be nice if we're together here in Barnesville?"

He laughed straight out. "Of course it would be.

The best thing that could happen in an already perfect world."

"Then stop this fretting and accept my gift to you. Daisy and I are moving here, and that's it, end of discussion."

"One thing living with three women has taught me is to know when to throw in the towel. Thank you."

"You're welcome."

His kiss was incredible, soft and hot at the same time, and when it ended Gillian could hardly breathe. Andrew's slow smile echoed the overwhelming love she felt, and she knew she was doing the right thing.

If Daisy had refused to leave the city and move to Barnesville, Gillian would never have considered returning to her childhood hometown. But in this case it was the daughter who wanted that move.

Andrew and his career weren't more important than hers, Gilly believed, but his family was. She had no one else but Daisy, but he had his parents and sisters who needed him close by. And, if she were completely honest with herself, she kind of liked the thought of having the wonderful Alma and her hardworking husband near, and of being able to sit in their cozy kitchen every other day, especially if she and Andrew were to have more children. No one would love their grandchildren more than Alma and Tom.

There was only one more thing for her to do before she could leave the past behind and concentrate on their future—she had to tell Andrew about Daisy.

Reluctantly she left his lap and sat facing him again. Confused, he leaned back, not understanding her sudden withdrawal.

"Before we decide anything, there is one last thing

I need to talk to you about," she said nervously. "Do you remember our senior prom?"

He visibly stiffened. "I do."

"If I remember it correctly, I think I need to apologize to you for behaving quite awfully toward you that evening. I more or less ditched you as soon as we got there, in pursuit of Luke."

"It's all right." He glanced away briefly, and his breathing seemed uncomfortable. "I got over it."

Raising her eyebrows, she stared at him in surprise. "You did?"

If there ever had been a sheepish smile, it was the one he gave her as he looked up at her. "No. Not really. There I was with my grand plans for the evening, and you ruined them all the moment we arrived. But to look on it from the bright side, I learned to never put all my cards on one horse."

"Are you calling me a horse?"

His hearty laughter filled the room. "No. Not now, at least. I might have back then."

This conversation was, as always when it came to Andrew, sidetracked. Usually Gillian didn't mind, she liked his way of always seeing things differently. But not now, not when she had something important to share with him, and the more he unknowingly stalled her news, the more she feared what his reaction would be.

"Anyway, I got drunk that night. Really drunk."

"I would say you were pretty drunk, yes."

"I don't have many memories from the party, but the thing I do know is that when I woke up the next morning I had lost more than my pride, I had also lost my virginity."

He paled, but for once he kept quiet, letting her continue without a joke or a clever input.

"All these years I've thought it had to have been Luke, because he was the one I would have done anything for, especially when drunk. But when I learned he was my brother…"

"Oh, Gillian." Andrew's compassion washed over her as he reached out, grabbing her cold hands. "How awful for you, thinking you'd had sex with your brother."

"It was. And that was why I was so shocked the other day, when you found me lying on the lawn. My whole world was going to pieces, and all I needed then was to talk to Luke, to learn if he had been the one. But he confessed he hadn't."

"You really don't remember?"

She shook her head. "No. When I asked Candice and Mrs. Cooper about that night, if they had seen me with someone, they both recollected me dancing quite closely with Matthew Barnes."

"Gillian…"

"The thought that it could have been he, one of the few persons in the world I just can't stand, made me nauseous." She knew she had cut him off, but she needed to do this in her way, at her pace. She didn't need him to blurt the truth out before she was ready. "But then it hit me: why would I have let him so close to me? I could hardly stand him, loathed him for how he behaved toward Megan. No, that was so not me. I would only have opened up for someone I loved, someone I trusted. And as Luke was already ruled out, the only one it could have been…was you."

He stared at their entwined hands, as if he was too

embarrassed to meet her eyes. "I'm so sorry, Gillian. I never meant it to happen, but I wasn't used to alcohol, and I was so wired up with emotions for you that when you wanted me to hug you and comfort you because you felt abandoned, I just had to kiss you. A little. But your mouth was so sweet, and when you kissed me back… I know it's not an excuse, but I loved you too much to stop. Afterwards I felt awful, and when you didn't remember anything… Well, I was so ashamed over what I had done to you—and don't you give me that look. It *was* my fault, because your willingness was because of the alcohol. And yes, I was drunk too, but not that drunk. I knew exactly what I was doing and could have stopped anytime, but I didn't. In the end I decided not to tell you, to give you a chance to reconcile with Luke."

He let go of her hands and ran his fingers through his hair. She knew she was acting the ogre, forcing him to open up like this, but she needed the whole story from him before she told him about the result of their lovemaking.

"It all changed when I learned Luke had left Barnesville without any thought of returning. I knew then we were meant to be together. Why else would the only obstacle in our way leave the road open? So I tried to talk to you, but you kept rambling on about Luke this and Luke that, told me all about how much you had to see him, and I just couldn't make myself tell you to shut up and listen to me instead. So I went home, still with my secret intact."

"And then your father hurt his back."

He looked at her with surprise. "Yes, as a matter of fact he did. I got caught up with all his chores at the farm, and when I finally had a chance to go and see you again, you were gone. You never even said goodbye. You just walked out, turned your back on everything and everyone. On me."

"I had no choice."

She could see he didn't understand and knew this was the moment to let him know the whole truth about her.

"My mother threw me out of the house, ordering me to get as far away from Barnesville as I could and never come back again."

"What? She threw you out? B-but...why? Why would Rachel throw you out?"

"Because I was pregnant."

"You were pr..."

His voice trailed off as he tried to make sense of what she was telling him. He still hadn't figured out his own involvement, that was quite clear, and she waited patiently but with more and more excitement every second.

"But why would Rachel throw you out because of a pregnancy? She was one of the most traditional people I knew, always lecturing about the importance of family and genes."

"Yes. But it all changed when she thought Luke was the father, the same Luke she hadn't bothered to tell me was my brother."

"Oh, Lord."

"So she gave me whatever money she had at home and pushed me out. I was eighteen years old, pregnant, and too scared to think straight."

"But it wasn't Luke who was the father, it was me, and I..."

And there the penny finally fell. With an astonished look, Andrew leaned back in the chair, his handsome face slowly starting to glow as the truth settled in. Sheer happiness poured out through every pore of his body as he looked at her with amazement.

"Daisy's mine."

"Yes."

"I'm the father she has been seeking."

"No."

He frowned. "No?"

"No, she stopped looking a while ago when she realized it was you."

"She did?"

"Uh-hum."

"Clever girl."

"Got it from her father."

"Yes…" Tears filled his eyes as the meaning of her words came to him, and she couldn't stand the distance anymore. Without a word she got up and put herself in his lap, her most favorite place in all the world. With a sob, he hid his face in the crook of her neck, and she hugged him tightly as his large body trembled with his crying.

"You know," she said softly as she stroked his blond hair. "I always thought her father had to be dark-haired because my family is blond and Daisy is not. I think that's why I didn't consider you at first. But the more I think about it, the more I realize she's just like you. Just as honest, open, and adventurous. Do you remember when you first met her outside your office, the day we arrived? You two hit it off immediately, talking exactly the same language. She has never liked anyone as quickly as she did you."

His voice was muffled, with his mouth pressed against her neck, but she heard what he said anyway. "My father used to have dark hair, but it turned gray early. All because of me and my sisters, he has assured us many times."

"I didn't know that. I just remembered his light hair. There, you see? She's the spitting image of your father's hair."

His shoulders shook with laughter as he sat up and without shame dried his puffy eyes. "God, I wish I'd had the guts back then, when it all happened. Then you two would have been mine all along."

"But you didn't, and I left. So let's just scratch the past. Instead, we can concentrate on the future. *Our* future, which the three of us are going to spend together. You, me, and our obnoxious daughter."

"She's a handful, that's for sure."

"But now I've got you to take care of it all, and I can just lean back and enjoy the good parts instead."

Laughing, he hugged her close, too happy to know what to say. So he kissed her instead. An almost holy, sacred kiss, but she didn't mind. She too thought this moment was special.

Finally she was home, where she belonged. No more secrets. No more lies. The road ahead lay open and inviting, and she could hardly wait to start walking down it, with Andrew's large hand in hers.

The voices in the kitchen grew louder as Andrew's sisters and Daisy arrived, ready to eat lunch, and she could see how his daughter's sweet voice filled him with happiness.

"I love you, Silly Gilly House Mouse."

"And I love you. Now go and tell your daughter to

stop disturbing your mother. I'm hungry."

Again his warm laughter filled the air, and she closed her eyes as he lifted her off his lap and hastened toward the kitchen, eager to meet the girl he now knew was his daughter.

With a happy sigh, Gillian stood up, but instead of following him, she went to the window and looked out over the billowing fields outside. Andrew's words about Rachel's reaction to the news of Gillian's return had healed a few of the scars in her heart.

Just knowing her mother had looked forward to her arrival at first soothed the turbulence in her heart and made it easier for her to accept the truth.

Her mother had loved her in her own way.

Rachel would never have said it out loud, would not have even hinted to Gillian about it, but it didn't matter anymore. The truth was out, and finally she could put her old life behind and grasp the future instead.

Daisy's light voice was heard from the kitchen, and the sound made Gillian smile with satisfaction. Her daughter was happy and content, well assured that her mother loved her more than life. It was all Gillian had ever wanted herself, and to be able to give her own daughter the security of a parent's unconditional love was like manna for her.

"Gillian!" Andrew's laughing voice made her shake the sentimental thoughts away, and with light steps she walked toward the kitchen and the family who awaited her, eager to start the journey toward the rest of her life.

A word about the author...

Mother of kids. Writer of romance. Addict of coffee.

www.jenniferwenn.com

Books by Jennifer Wenn
available from The Wild Rose Press, Inc.
The Royal Family Regency series...
A FAMILY AFFAIR
NEVER HAD A DREAM COME TRUE
THE BEAUTY OF YOU
...with more to come.
The Barnesville contemporary series...
ALWAYS YOU
A FATHER FOR DAISY
...with more to come.